# THE ALPHA DEPUTY

## A SMALL-TOWN OMEGAVERSE FATED MATES ROMANCE

### ASH JADE

D ear Reader,

Welcome to Sanctuary, a hidden mountain town whispered about in the wider omegaverse, a place where worn-down omegas come to heal and alphas learn that strength is measured in gentleness, not dominance. If you've made it this far, maybe part of you is curious... or hopeful... or simply ready to step into a world where instinct doesn't have to hurt, and where every story bends toward safety, connection, and a well-earned happily-ever-after.

Here, the omegaverse works a little differently.

Alphas, betas, and omegas still move through life guided by pheromones, instincts, and bonds, but Sanctuary is a refuge, one carved out of grief, rebuilt with stubborn hope, and held together by a pack that refuses to let anyone fall through the cracks. Heats and ruts still come like wild weather, but they're met with care, consent, and hands that steady instead of seize. And sometimes, the mountain air carries something more ancient still: the pull of fated mates, that quiet click inside your chest when you realize home might be a person as much as a place.

Each novella in this series is a fast, high-heat, heart-forward escape. A story about a protective alpha, a brave omega, and the slow re-teaching of trust. You can read them in order or wander in wherever you like. Every couple stands alone, yet each book threads another stitch into the found-family tapestry of Sanctuary.

Before you step inside, a few gentle warnings:

These stories contain explicit sexual content, primal dynamics, instinct-driven tension, and adult themes. They are not dark romance, but they *do* explore trauma recovery, vulnerability, and the process of learning to choose yourself again. Please honor your comfort level and step away if something doesn't sit right with you.

Additional content considerations: violence, injury, death, mentions of sexual violence (not depicted but discussed), and themes of healing from past harm.

If Sanctuary sounds like somewhere you might want to linger—if you're ready for protective alphas, fierce omegas, small-town gossip, soft pack dinners, and bonds that bloom where hurt once lived—then settle in.

The mountains are waiting.

— Ash Jade

# Contents


1. Chapter 1     1

2. Chapter 2     7

3. Chapter 3     13

4. Chapter 4     21

5. Chapter 5     28

6. Chapter 6     35

7. Chapter 7     43

8. Chapter 8     54

9. Chapter 9     62

10. Chapter 10     70

11. Chapter 11     78

12. Chapter 12     86

13. Chapter 13     98

Bonus Epilogue     106

Also by Ash Jade     113

About Ash Jade     116

# 1

I kneel down to Tommy's eye level, putting myself between him and Zack, who's nursing a bloody lip and glaring daggers over my shoulder. The playground asphalt bites into my knees through my thin skirt, but I barely notice. Kindergarteners have surprisingly effective right hooks when properly motivated.

"Tommy," I say, keeping my voice steady despite the chaos of twenty-four other five-year-olds circling like tiny vultures, "we use our words, not our fists, remember?"

Tommy's lower lip trembles. His sandy blond hair is sticking up in tufts from where Zack grabbed it. "He said my mom left 'cause I'm bad."

My heart cracks a little. Sanctuary is full of broken stories—omegas fleeing dangerous situations, children bearing the weight of adult cruelty. I take Tommy's small hands in mine. "That's not true. And it hurt to hear, didn't it?"

He nods, tears welling.

"But hurting Zack back doesn't fix that hurt inside you." I turn to Zack, whose defiant pose doesn't quite hide his fear. "And Zack, words can cut deeper than fists. Tommy's mom loves him very much. She just can't be here right now."

Zack's eyes drop to the ground. The tang of shame-sweat rises from his skin—a child's scent is so unguarded, so honest. I'm about to guide them through an apology when a wave of alpha pheromones slams into me like a physical force.

The children feel it too. Their little bodies tense and huddle closer to me, instinct driving them to seek protection from an omega. I straighten up, my spine stiffening as a Sanctuary Sheriff's Department SUV pulls up to the curb.

Deputy Finn Donovan unfolds from the driver's seat like a switchblade—all sharp edges and controlled danger. He stalks toward us, aviators hiding his eyes but doing nothing to diminish the force of his presence. His uniform stretches across broad shoulders, gun holstered at his hip. The children shrink behind me.

"What seems to be the problem here?" His voice is gravel and whiskey, a rough-edged rumble that carries across the playground. Parents at the fence are watching now, their conversation dying as they sense the shift in atmosphere.

I step forward, placing myself firmly between him and my students. "There's no problem, Deputy.

Just a minor disagreement between children that we've already resolved."

His nostrils flare slightly—he's scenting me, the arrogant ass. "Got a call about a fight. Blood drawn." He gestures toward Zack's lip, which has indeed left a small red stain on his shirt collar.

"A scratch. I'm handling it."

The deputy's jaw tightens. "School policy requires law enforcement notification for physical altercations."

"They're five, Deputy Donovan. Not hardened criminals." I keep my voice sweet, but there's steel underneath. The parents are drawing closer now, scenting the confrontation between alpha and omega.

"Rules are rules, Miss Wilson." He peers over his sunglasses, and I get my first real look at his eyes—amber with flecks of gold, like whiskey held to sunlight. Something electric passes between us, a recognition that has nothing to do with our professional interaction.

I break the connection first. "And context matters. These children need guidance, not intimidation."

He steps closer, lowering his voice. "Are you suggesting I can't tell the difference?"

His scent washes over me—cedar and smooke, like storm clouds gathering over mountains. My omega hindbrain traitorously purrs, recognizing his strength, the protection he could offer. I ruthlessly shove that reaction deep down where it belongs.

"I'm suggesting that your presence is making them afraid, not helping them learn."

A flash of something—hurt? surprise?—crosses his face before the professional mask slams back down. "Fear of consequences is a perfectly reasonable deterrent, Miss Wilson."

"For adults who understand those consequences, perhaps. For children still learning emotional regulation?" I gesture to Tommy, who's practically trying to crawl inside my cardigan at this point. "Look at them, Deputy. Really look."

For a moment, he does. I see his expression shift as he takes in their wide eyes, their small bodies trembling with instinctive fear of a dominant alpha. Something softens in his posture.

"Miss Jenny's right." The voice comes from behind me—Olivia Rawlins, the sheriff's mate and the school's newly appointed principal, approaching with quiet authority. Her presence eases some of the tension. Even Deputy Donovan seems to defer slightly to her. "Finn, I think Miss Wilson has this well in hand."

He hesitates, jaw working. I can practically see him battling between his alpha instinct to assert dominance and his better judgment.

"I'll file the incident report myself," I offer, professional but firm.

After a long moment, he nods curtly. "See that you do." He turns to the children, and his voice drops an octave, gentler but still firm. "Fighting is never the answer, boys. Next time, find a teacher."

As he walks away, I feel the collective relief from twenty-six kindergarteners—and if I'm honest, from me too, though for entirely different reasons. His alpha presence set something humming under my skin, a response I haven't felt in years. Dangerous territory for an omega who's fought hard for her independence.

"You stood up to him," Olivia murmurs, impressed. "Not many people challenge Finn Donovan."

I watch his broad back as he returns to his vehicle, the set of his shoulders rigid with frustration. "Someone should. That man needs to learn that authority isn't just about intimidation."

She laughs softly. "Perhaps. Or perhaps he needs someone who isn't afraid of his bark."

I turn back to my class, clapping my hands to regain their attention. "Alright, everyone! Circle time on the grass. Tommy and Zack, please shake hands first."

As I lead my line of children toward our usual spot, I can't help glancing back. Deputy Donovan hasn't left yet. He's watching me from behind his sunglasses, a curious expression on his face. When our eyes meet, he doesn't look away.

Neither do I.

Something tells me this won't be our last clash. The thought sends a thrill racing down my spine—half warning, half anticipation.

**2**

— · —

I catch myself sniffing my cardigan sleeve for the third time today. His scent—cedar and smoke—clings to the fabric like a stubborn memory. I yank my arm down, furious with myself. One run-in with Deputy Hard-Ass and I'm what—scenting my clothes like some touch-starved omega? Pathetic.

"Miss Jenny, I made you a flower!" Lily pushes a crumpled tissue paper creation into my hand, mercifully interrupting my spiral.

I smile, tucking away thoughts of amber eyes and broad shoulders. "It's beautiful. Should we add it to our spring wall?"

The classroom hums with afternoon energy—twenty-six kindergarteners cutting, pasting, and chattering as they finish their art projects. This is my domain. My sanctuary. No room here for thoughts of infuriating alphas who think fear makes better lessons than understanding.

"Five minutes until clean-up time," I announce, circling the tables, admiring lopsided paper flowers and helping small fingers with scissors. A flash of movement through the window catches my eye—a sheriff's department SUV pulling into the parking lot.

My stomach twists. Surely he wouldn't…

The rest of the afternoon drags like feet through wet cement. By the time the last parent collects their child, my nerves are frayed. I gather my tote bag, bursting with papers to grade and tomorrow's lesson plans, and lock my classroom door with more force than necessary.

The late afternoon sun slants across the playground as I exit through the side door. And there he is—leaning against his SUV, arms crossed over his chest, mirrored aviators hiding his eyes. Waiting. For me.

I consider turning around. Taking the back exit. But that would be retreating, and Jenny Wilson doesn't retreat.

"Deputy Donovan," I call, approaching with my chin lifted. "Checking for playground brawlers again?"

His mouth—an irritatingly well-shaped mouth—quirks up at one corner. "Miss Wilson. I'm following up on yesterday's incident report. The one you were supposed to file."

Shit. I'd meant to, really. But Tommy had needed extra attention after school, and then prep for today had taken longer than expected...

"It's on my desk. I'll email it to the station tonight." I shift my heavy tote to my other shoulder. "Was that worth a special trip?"

He pushes off the SUV, taking off those ridiculous glasses. His eyes are even more unsettling in the golden afternoon light—amber and predatory. "Sheriff wanted me to check the school's security protocols while I was here. Two birds, one stone."

"How efficient." I move to walk past him, but he steps sideways, blocking my path.

"You disagree with how I handled yesterday." Not a question.

I look up at him—he's unfairly tall, forcing me to crane my neck. "You scared children who were already upset. So yes, I disagreed."

"Sometimes a little fear is educational."

"Is that how you were raised, Deputy? Fear as a teaching tool?"

Something flickers behind his eyes—a shadow of something old and painful. It's gone so quickly I almost think I imagined it.

"Structure and consequences," he says, voice lower. "The world doesn't coddle people, Miss Wilson. Better they learn that young."

"There's a difference between coddling and compassion." I take a step closer, my omega instincts be damned. "Those children are learning how to be people. Some of them have only ever known fear as a motivator. I won't add to that."

The air between us charges with something dangerous—not just the clash of our philosophies but something more primal. His scent intensifies, wrapping around me like smoke from a wildfire. Cedar and heat and something wilder underneath. My body responds before my brain can shut it down, releasing a soft wave of omega response.

His nostrils flare. Pupils dilate.

"You think I don't care about those kids." His voice has dropped an octave, rougher now.

"I think you care about order more than understanding."

"And you understand everything, do you?" He steps closer. Too close. "Every broken child, every mess, every damaged soul that washes up in this town?"

"I try." My voice wavers despite my best efforts. "Which is more than most people do."

For a heartbeat—just one—his expression softens. The cynical mask slips, revealing something raw and vulnerable beneath. A man, not just a badge. It knocks the air from my lungs more effectively than any alpha posturing.

Then it's gone, shuttered away. He steps back, clearing his throat.

"Your incident report. Tonight." He slides his glasses back on, all professional distance once more. "And lock the side gate. It was open when I arrived."

I nod, suddenly exhausted by our clash. "Anything else, Deputy?"

"Yeah." He pauses, hand on his car door. "Not all protection looks soft, Miss Wilson."

Before I can respond, he's folded his tall frame into the SUV and pulled away, leaving me standing in a swirl of dust and confusion.

Later, in my small rental cottage on the edge of town, I sit on my porch swing with a glass of wine and curse his existence. The wine is cheap, my feet are bare, and the spring night hums with cricket song.

"Arrogant, condescending alpha," I mutter to no one. My cat, Mabel, blinks at me from the porch railing, unimpressed.

But even as I rail against him in my mind, I can't forget that single moment of vulnerability. The way his scent clung to my cardigan—which I definitely did not sniff again after hanging it up. The intensity in his eyes when he told me not all protection looks soft.

I drain my glass and close my eyes, letting the porch swing rock gently.

He's everything I've fought against—alphas who think they know best, who use their strength to intimidate rather than protect. Dominance without understanding.

So why can't I stop replaying that moment when his eyes softened? Why does his scent linger in my memory like a song I can't stop humming?

And why, despite my better judgment, do I feel the strangest pull to see him again?

**3**

—·—

"You'll be working with Deputy Donovan on the new safety protocols," Olivia says, her smile a touch too innocent as she drops this bomb in my lap during our Monday morning staff meeting. The other teachers' heads swivel toward me in perfect unison, their expressions ranging from sympathy to poorly concealed amusement. My coffee cup freezes halfway to my lips. Working with Deputy Hard-Ass? The universe has a sick sense of humor.

"Surely there are other deputies," I manage, setting my cup down before I spill it.

Olivia's eyes sparkle with mischief. "Sheriff Rawlins feels Deputy Donovan's expertise in crisis management makes him the ideal candidate. And after your... passionate exchange last week, I thought you might have some valuable perspectives to share."

Valuable perspectives. Right. Like how his alpha posturing makes my skin crawl. Or how his scent haunts me for days after each encounter. Or how I've replayed our arguments in my head like favorite songs on repeat.

"When do we start?" My voice sounds strangled even to my own ears.

"First community meeting is Thursday evening." She slides a folder toward me. "You'll find the agenda and initial proposals inside. I expect you to play nice, Jenny."

Play nice. As if I'm the problem. As if I'm the one who shows up with a gun on my hip and fear tactics in my pocket.

"Of course," I say with my brightest, fakest kindergarten teacher smile. "We're all professionals here."

I arrive at Town Hall thirty minutes early on Thursday, determined to stake my territory before Deputy Donovan arrives. The community room smells of floor wax and stale coffee. I arrange my notes meticulously, setting up a display board with photos of our school's current safety measures and a list of proposed improvements that won't turn our playground into a prison yard.

The door swings open ten minutes before the meeting. I don't need to look up to know it's him—his scent reaches me first, that maddening mix of cedar and smoke that makes my hindbrain sit up and take notice.

"Miss Wilson." He nods curtly, surveying my setup with narrowed eyes.

"Deputy." I straighten, smoothing my floral dress. I deliberately wore my brightest colors today—a silent rebellion against his perpetual uniform of intimidation.

He sets his own materials on the opposite end of the table—all graphs and security protocols printed in stark black and white. No surprise there.

People begin filtering in—parents, other teachers, town council members. I recognize most of them; Sanctuary isn't big enough for strangers. Mrs. Landry from the bakery winks at me as she takes a seat. Old Mr. Peterson from the hardware store settles in with a knowing smile.

Olivia calls the meeting to order, explaining the initiative to create updated safety protocols for the school. "We're fortunate to have both Miss Wilson and Deputy Donovan leading this effort—bringing together perspectives from both education and law enforcement."

I step forward first, outlining my vision: "Safety isn't just about locks and drills. It's about creating an environment where children feel secure enough to learn and grow. Where they know adults will protect them without frightening them."

I discuss trauma-informed approaches, the importance of maintaining a nurturing atmosphere, how fear impacts developing brains.

When I finish, Finn stands, command radiating from his posture.

"With all due respect to Miss Wilson's... idealism," he starts, making me bristle, "security requires structure. Clear protocols. Enforceable boundaries."

He launches into statistics about school incidents nationwide, showing diagrams of security checkpoints and evacuation routes. His voice carries the weight of absolute certainty.

"Children need to understand how to respond in emergencies," he says. "That means realistic drills, not sugar-coated scenarios."

I interrupt before I can stop myself. "And traumatizing five-year-olds accomplishes what, exactly?"

His jaw tightens. "Preparing them for realities they might face."

"By teaching them the world is a dangerous place they should fear?"

"Instead of pretending it's not?"

We're facing each other now, the rest of the room forgotten. I catch the scent of his frustration—sharper, spicier than his usual cedar notes. It sparks something in me, a compulsion to push further.

"There's a difference between preparation and paranoia, Deputy."

"And between protection and negligence, Miss Wilson."

Olivia clears her throat loudly. "Perhaps we should hear from some parents?"

The spell breaks. I become aware of the room again—of the barely suppressed smiles, the exchanged glances. Mrs. Landry is covering her mouth, shoulders shaking with silent laughter. Mr. Peterson looks like he's watching his favorite sport.

For the rest of the meeting, Finn and I maintain frigid professionalism, though I feel his eyes on me each time I speak. The air between us crackles with unresolved tension.

The second meeting goes no better. If anything, the town seems more entertained by our clashes. We're becoming a spectacle—the stubborn deputy and the defiant teacher. Olivia pulls me aside afterward.

"You two need to find common ground," she says. "This isn't helping anyone, least of all the children."

I want to argue, but she's right. Still, something about Finn Donovan gets under my skin like no one else. The way he stands—legs braced apart, hands on his belt, every inch the dominant alpha. The way his voice drops when he's making a point he believes in passionately. The way his eyes track my movements when he thinks I'm not looking.

The third meeting shifts something. We're discussing emergency response protocols when Finn unexpectedly backs one of my suggestions.

"Miss Wilson's point about having comfort items in the safe rooms has merit," he says, surprising everyone, including me. "Children process fear differently. Having familiar objects could help maintain calm during lockdown situations."

I stare at him, momentarily speechless. He meets my eyes directly, and for a brief, disorienting moment, we're allies instead of adversaries.

"Thank you," I say, voice softer than intended.

Something passes between us—recognition, maybe. The faintest acknowledgment that neither of us is entirely wrong. His scent changes subtly, the smoky notes mellowing into something warmer.

Then Mrs. Hernandez asks about armed resource officers, and we're back to opposite corners, arguing our positions with renewed vigor.

But that moment lingers. Even as we debate, I find myself watching his hands, the way they gesture when he's making a point. The curve of his neck when he bends to examine a document. The small scar on his jaw that I hadn't noticed before.

After the fourth meeting devolves into another heated exchange, the town council president throws up his hands.

"Enough," he says. "You two are going to co-lead a presentation at next month's town hall. One cohesive proposal that incorporates both perspectives. Figure it out."

My stomach drops. Weeks of working closely with Finn. Planning. Compromising. Existing in each other's space.

"Fine," Finn says, jaw tight.

"Of course," I echo, not looking at him.

As we gather our materials, our hands brush. A jolt of awareness travels up my arm. His scent sharpens, and I know he felt it too.

"My office or yours?" he asks, voice deliberately neutral.

"The school would be better. We should work in the actual environment we're planning for."

He nods once, curtly. "Tomorrow after your classes?"

"Four o'clock," I confirm.

Walking to my car afterward, I can't decide whether to be furious or thrilled. Forced proximity to an alpha who challenges everything I believe. Who gets under my skin like no one else. Whose scent makes my omega instincts stir despite my better judgment.

This is a disaster waiting to happen. So why am I already counting the hours until tomorrow?

# 4

The first planning session with Finn goes better than expected and worse than I'd hoped. Better because we actually make progress on our presentation. Worse because three hours in a classroom with him leaves me dizzy with his scent, hyperaware of his every movement. Each time he leans over my shoulder to look at my notes, heat radiates between us like a physical entity. By the time he leaves, my skin feels too tight, my nerves raw and exposed. I tell myself it's just biology—alpha and omega proximity, nothing more. The lie tastes bitter on my tongue.

I spend the night restless, my dreams filled with amber eyes and the phantom scent of cedar. I wake tangled in sheets, body humming with an ache I refuse to name.

Our second meeting is scheduled for Thursday after school. I stay late, preparing the classroom, arranging my notes in meticulous piles. My stomach flutters with something that isn't quite dread. At four-fifteen, a knock on my door.

But it's not Finn who steps into my classroom.

"Deputy Ramirez," I say, unable to hide my surprise. "I was expecting Deputy Donovan."

Ramirez shifts uncomfortably, his beta scent mild and inoffensive compared to Finn's overwhelming alpha presence. "He got pulled into another assignment. Asked me to drop off these security specs and work with you today."

My smile feels brittle. "Of course. Please, have a seat."

We work for two hours. Ramirez is competent, polite, and entirely wrong for this project. He doesn't challenge me. Doesn't push back when I suggest modifications to the lockdown protocols. Doesn't make my skin tingle when he hands me a document.

It's infuriating how much I miss the clash.

The next meeting, it's Deputy Chen. Then Officer Michaels. By the third Finn-less meeting, it's obvious—he's avoiding me. Deliberately and thoroughly.

I tell myself I'm relieved. Working with other officers is certainly easier on my blood pressure. My concentration. My inconvenient omega biology that responds to his alpha presence like a tuning fork struck at the perfect frequency.

But the relief never comes. Instead, a hollow ache takes root beneath my breastbone—a persistent, nagging discomfort that worsens with each day he stays away.

I spot him at Marge's Diner on a rainy Tuesday, hunched over coffee at the counter. I've stopped in for my usual post-school caffeine, and the sight of his broad shoulders makes my steps falter. His head turns slightly—he's scented me—but he doesn't look back. His body language screams avoidance.

Before I can overthink it, I march up beside him.

"Deputy Donovan," I say brightly, sliding onto the adjacent stool. "Fancy meeting you here."

His jaw tightens, a muscle jumping beneath tanned skin. "Miss Wilson."

"I've been working with half your department lately. I was beginning to think you'd skipped town."

He takes a deliberate sip of coffee, still not meeting my eyes. "Been busy."

"Too busy for our presentation? The one due in two weeks?"

Finally, he looks at me. The impact of those amber eyes after days without them hits like a physical blow. My omega whines with pathetic joy at the attention.

"The others have been keeping me updated. Your ideas are... not bad."

I arch an eyebrow. "High praise, coming from you."

Something flickers across his face—discomfort, maybe. Or hunger. He shifts on his stool, putting another inch of distance between us.

"Chen says you've got the evacuation routes redesigned."

"I do." I lean closer, deliberately invading the space he's trying to create. "But you'd know that if you'd shown up."

His nostrils flare. I watch his throat work as he swallows. The air between us thickens, charged with something dangerous.

"I should go," he says abruptly, throwing cash on the counter. "Got a shift."

"Run along then, Deputy." I keep my tone light, teasing, hiding the irrational hurt beneath. "Some of us will actually finish the work."

He pauses, half-standing, something raw in his expression. For a heartbeat, I think he might say something real. Then his professional mask slams back into place.

"Tomorrow, four o'clock. I'll be there."

He strides out without looking back. I watch him go, the ache in my chest intensifying until I press my palm against my sternum, trying to soothe it. Marge slides a coffee in front of me, her knowing eyes too perceptive.

"That boy's running scared," she says, wiping the counter with a practiced swipe.

"From what?" I ask, though I'm afraid I already know.

She just smiles, moving down the counter to her next customer.

Later that night, I do what I swore I wouldn't—I research mate bonds. My laptop screen glows in the darkness of my living room as I scroll through medical sites, omega forums, even some dubious mystical blogs.

*Increased scent awareness.* Check.

*Physical discomfort when separated.* The ache in my chest says yes.

*Heightened awareness of the other's presence.* God, yes.

*Dreams and intrusive thoughts.* Embarrassingly yes.

I slam the laptop closed, pressing the heels of my hands against my eyes. This can't be happening. Mate bonds are rare. Practically mythical. The stuff of romance novels and teenage fantasies.

And even if they were real—which I'm not convinced they are—they wouldn't happen to me. Not with him. The universe wouldn't be that cruel.

I've built my life on independence. On choices freely made. The idea that some biological imperative could override my carefully constructed autonomy is terrifying.

And yet...

I think of his scent—how it cuts through everything else, wrapping around me like a physical touch. How my body orients toward him in a room without conscious thought. How the sight of him sends electricity dancing across my skin.

The emptiness when he stays away.

I press my palm against my chest again, feeling the persistent ache that's become my constant companion. Is this what those websites meant? This hollow, hungry feeling that nothing seems to fill?

Mabel jumps onto the couch beside me, her small warm body pressing against my thigh. I stroke her absently, lost in thought.

"It's not a mate bond," I tell her firmly. "It's just... chemistry. Biological compatibility. It doesn't mean anything."

She blinks at me, unimpressed with my denial.

"Fine," I mutter. "It's attraction. I'm attracted to a man who represents everything I've fought against. Happy now?"

But even as I say it, I know it's more than attraction. Attraction doesn't make your chest ache when they're gone. Doesn't make their scent linger in your memory like a haunting melody. Doesn't make you feel like a piece of yourself is missing when they avoid you.

I curl up on my side, Mabel nestling against me, and stare at the shadows on my ceiling. The rain patters against my roof, a gentle, persistent rhythm.

What if it is real? What if fate, or biology, or whatever force creates these bonds has tied me to Finn Donovan? The thought should terrify me. Instead, beneath the fear and resistance, a small, treacherous part of me whispers:

What if we're meant to be?

**5**

I first hear it from Marge while grabbing my morning coffee—a whisper of concern wrapped in the usual small-town gossip.

"You be careful at that school, honey," she says, sliding my latte across the counter. "Sheriff's had three reports of someone watching the playground. Probably nothing, but..."

She trails off, but her eyes—sharp as ever—tell me she's genuinely worried. My fingers tighten around the cardboard cup, the protective instinct for my students flaring like a sudden fever.

"Who reported it?" I ask, keeping my voice casual though my pulse has already quickened.

"Mrs. Abernathy saw someone in the woods behind the jungle gym yesterday. Said he ducked away when she noticed him. Then the crossing guard spotted someone taking pictures from a car." She leans closer, lowering her voice. "Sheriff's taking it seriously. Increasing patrols."

I nod, thanking her for the warning. As I walk to my car, I scan the street with new awareness, cataloging unfamiliar vehicles, watching for faces that don't belong.

Sanctuary has always been safe—that's the point, the reason so many omegas come here seeking refuge from dangerous situations. The thought of that sanctuary being violated makes my skin crawl.

At school, I find myself pausing at the windows more often, gaze drawn to the tree line beyond the playground. The morning passes in a blur of alphabet songs and counting games, but my attention remains split—one part teacher, one part sentinel.

During recess, I position myself at the edge of the playground, closer to the woods than usual. The children's laughter rings in the crisp spring air as they chase each other across the blacktop, blissfully unaware of any threat. I intend to keep it that way.

A flicker of movement catches my eye—something shifting between the pines at the forest edge. I step forward, straining to see. For a moment, I make out a dark figure, watching. Our eyes meet across the distance, and a chill slides down my spine like ice water.

Then the figure retreats, melting back into the shadows.

I report it immediately to Olivia, who calls the sheriff's office. By afternoon, a patrol car sits prominently in the school parking lot. It should make me feel better. Instead, the visible reminder of danger only heightens my anxiety.

Over the next two days, I implement my own security measures in my classroom—keeping the blinds drawn, positioning myself between the door and my students, creating a "quiet corner" where children can retreat if they feel scared without knowing the real reason for its existence. I stay later each evening, checking window locks, scanning the treeline before leaving.

On the third day, Finn shows up in my classroom doorway just as I'm dismissing my students. His expression is thunderous, jaw tight, eyes flashing with barely contained fury. He waits—rigid and silent—until the last child has been collected.

The moment we're alone, he closes the door with controlled precision that somehow feels more threatening than a slam.

"You saw him." Not a question. "Yesterday, at the edge of the woods."

I straighten the already neat pile of papers on my desk, refusing to be intimidated. "Yes."

"And you approached him."

"I stepped closer to get a better look. I didn't leave the playground."

He paces the length of my classroom, all coiled energy and predatory grace. The scent of angry alpha fills the space—pine and smoke edged with something sharper, like ozone before lightning strikes. My omega instincts urge submission in the face of his obvious agitation. I ruthlessly suppress them.

"You need to stay home until we handle this," he says finally, turning to face me.

I blink, certain I've misheard. "Excuse me?"

"Until we identify and apprehend this individual, you should—"

"Hide?" I interrupt, incredulous. "Abandon my students?"

His nostrils flare. "We'll have a substitute."

"Absolutely not." I cross my arms over my chest. "These children need consistency, especially now. They need familiar faces, routines they can trust."

"What they need is to not have their teacher become a target." He steps closer, looming over me, using his height advantage deliberately. "He's watching you specifically, Jenny. Not just the school."

The use of my first name catches me off-guard. In all our clashes, he's never once called me Jenny.

"You don't know that," I say, but with less conviction.

"Yesterday, you stayed until six. He waited in the woods until your car left the lot. Then he approached your classroom windows."

Cold dread pools in my stomach. "How do you—"

"Because I was watching him watch you." His voice drops lower, vibrating with intensity. "He followed your car for three blocks before turning off."

I swallow hard, fighting the fear rising in my throat. "All the more reason for me to be here, with the children. If he's fixated on me, I don't want him approaching some substitute looking for information."

"Damnit, Jenny!" He slams his palm against my desk, making me jump. "For once in your life, can you not argue about every goddamn thing? This isn't a debate about playground rules. This is your safety."

Something in his expression stops my angry retort before it forms. Beneath the fury, behind the professional concern of a law enforcement officer, I see raw, naked fear. Not for the school, not for the children, but for me specifically. The realization knocks the breath from my lungs.

"I can't hide," I say more gently. "I won't. These kids—some of them have already experienced too much instability, too many adults disappearing from their lives without explanation. I won't be one more person who vanishes when things get difficult."

His jaw works as he struggles to maintain control. "Then at least let me assign someone to you. Chen can—"

"No. No escorts, no obvious security. That would only frighten the children."

"Then I'll do it myself." His voice leaves no room for argument. "I'll be in the parking lot at drop-off and pick-up. I'll patrol the perimeter during recess. I'll personally ensure you get home safely."

The thought of Finn watching over me, orbiting my day like a protective satellite, sends an unwelcome thrill through my body. I tamp it down, focusing on practicalities.

"Fine," I concede. "But you maintain a distance. No scaring my students with your angry alpha glare."

The corner of his mouth twitches—almost a smile. "I have other expressions."

"I've yet to see evidence of that."

The tension between us shifts, something softer threading through the conflict. For a moment, we're not adversaries but allies against a common threat.

The moment shatters with a sharp knock on my classroom door. Officer Chen pokes his head in, expression grim.

"Deputy, we found something. Outside Miss Wilson's window."

Finn's demeanor changes instantly, all business now. He follows Chen into the hallway while I trail behind, stomach knotting with dread.

On the ground beneath my classroom window lies a small, white stuffed rabbit. Identical to the one I keep on my desk—a gift from my first class of kindergarteners in Sanctuary. Except this one has been mutilated, its throat slashed, stuffing spilling out like blood, a crude note pinned to its chest. I can't read the words from here, but Finn's reaction tells me enough. His entire body goes rigid, a low growl building in his chest.

"Get her out of here," he orders Chen, not looking at me. "Take her straight to the station."

"I need to lock up my classroom," I protest weakly, my eyes fixed on the mangled toy.

"Now, Chen," Finn says, his voice a dangerous rumble. "Don't let her out of your sight."

As Chen guides me toward his cruiser, I glance back. Finn stands over the grotesque warning, his posture transformed into something primal and deadly. Gone is the cynical deputy with his rulebook and regulations. In his place stands a predator, an alpha ready to tear apart anything threatening what's his.

What's his.

The realization hits me with stunning clarity as Chen ushers me into the passenger seat. Finn doesn't just want to protect me because it's his job. He's reacting with the instinctive, visceral response of an alpha defending his mate.

Despite everything—the danger, the fear, the uncertainty—something warm unfurls in my chest. Something that feels dangerously like hope.

**6**

The first twinge hits as I'm erasing the whiteboard—a sudden flush of heat racing up my spine, pooling low in my belly. I freeze, marker suspended mid-air, recognizing the sensation with growing horror. No. Not now. Not here. My heats have always been regular, predictable—the next one isn't due for weeks. I press a shaking hand to my forehead, already slick with sweat. The classroom feels ten degrees warmer than it did moments ago, my cardigan suddenly suffocating against my skin.

I force myself to think through the rising fog. I need to get home. Need to secure myself before the heat takes over completely. Before my scent floods the hallways, broadcasting vulnerability to anyone nearby.

The marker clatters to the floor as another wave hits—stronger this time, stealing my breath. My knees buckle slightly, and I grab the edge of my desk. This isn't right. Heats build gradually, giving omegas time to prepare, to get somewhere safe. This is crashing through me like a freight train.

"Stress," I mutter to myself, trying to stay rational. "The threat. The lurker. The body's response to danger." And perhaps, though I don't want to admit it, proximity to a compatible alpha. To Finn.

I need to move. Now. Before I can't anymore.

I grab my bag with trembling hands, fumbling for my keys. They slip through my fingers, jingling against the tile floor. When I bend to retrieve them, dizziness washes over me in a nauseating wave. The room spins. My skin prickles with hypersensitivity, clothes abrasive against nerve endings suddenly tuned to maximum awareness.

Three more steps to the door. I can make it. Have to make it.

The hallway stretches before me, impossibly long. I'm conscious of wetness between my thighs, of my scent thickening in the air around me. Shame and arousal twist together in my gut as I stagger toward the exit. If I can just get to my car—

Another wave, stronger than the last. My vision blurs. I collide with the wall, bracing myself against the cool cinderblocks. My breath comes in short, desperate gasps.

I won't make it to the parking lot. Not like this.

I retreat to my classroom, locking the door behind me with fumbling fingers. Safe. At least temporarily. I sink into my chair, heat pulsing through me in relentless waves now. My phone. I need to call someone. Olivia, maybe. Another omega who would understand, who could help without being affected.

I reach for my bag, but it's across the room where I dropped it. The distance might as well be miles.

A sound from the hallway freezes me in place—footsteps. Heavy. Purposeful. A key in the lock.

The door swings open, and Finn stands frozen in the threshold, eyes widening as my scent hits him like a physical force. His nostrils flare, pupils dilating instantly. The door slams shut behind him.

"Jenny." My name sounds torn from his throat. Reverent and agonized.

I clutch the edge of my desk, mortification warring with the desperate, primal need surging through me. I want to hide, to disappear. I also want to throw myself at him, to beg for relief from this burning ache.

"You shouldn't be here," I manage, my voice a broken whisper.

He stays by the door, one hand white-knuckled on the knob, the other pressed flat against the wall as if physically restraining himself. His scent floods the room in response to mine—cedar and smoke intensified a hundredfold, with new notes of raw hunger and alpha arousal that make my inner omega whimper with need.

"I was checking the building," he says hoarsely. "Smelled you from the hallway."

Of course he did. My heat scent is probably detectable from the parking lot by now. Strong, unmistakable—broadcasting my fertility, my readiness, my desperation to every alpha in range.

To him specifically, my traitorous body seems to say, releasing another surge of pheromones that makes him growl low in his throat.

"You need to leave," I gasp, even as everything in me screams for him to come closer. "Please."

He doesn't move. His eyes—dark amber turned nearly black with desire—remain fixed on me. I can see the war raging within him—the alpha instinct to claim versus his human control.

"I can't leave you like this." His voice is rough, strained. "Not safe. Anyone could—" He cuts himself off, jaw clenching.

Another wave hits, more intense than the last. I cry out, unable to contain it, my body arching with need. Slick dampens my thighs, and Finn's response is immediate—a deep, rumbling growl that vibrates through the air between us.

"Call someone," he grates out. "Another omega. Someone who can get you home safely."

I shake my head, beyond coherent thought. "Phone... in my bag."

His eyes track to where my tote lies abandoned by the door. Without moving from his position, he stretches to hook it with his foot, sliding it toward me across the floor. Even this small consideration—keeping his distance when every instinct must be screaming at him to approach—pierces through the fog of my heat.

"Finn," I whisper, his name a plea for something I'm not sure I should want.

He closes his eyes briefly, as if in pain. "Don't. Don't say my name like that."

"Like what?" My voice sounds foreign to my own ears—husky, desperate.

"Like you want me to cross this room." His eyes open, blazing with restrained hunger. "Because if I do, Jenny, I don't know if I'll be able to stop."

The raw honesty in his voice cuts through some of the haze. This is Finn—stubborn, principled, infuriating Finn—fighting his most basic instincts to protect me. Even from himself.

I fumble for my phone with shaking hands, somehow managing to pull up Olivia's contact. She answers on the second ring.

"Jenny? Everything okay?"

"Heat," I choke out. "Early. At school. Need help."

I hear her sharp intake of breath, followed by immediate action. "Ten minutes. Stay put."

The call ends. I drop the phone, another wave of heat crashing over me. My skin feels too tight, too hot, too sensitive. Every nerve ending screams for relief, for touch, for him.

"Ten minutes," I pant, looking up at Finn. "Olivia's coming."

He nods once, jaw clenched so tight I can see the muscle jumping beneath his skin. He hasn't moved an inch from his position by the door.

"Talk to me," I plead, needing distraction from the fire consuming me. "Anything."

He swallows hard. "The threat. We identified him. Former alpha from a pack north of here. Had a claim on an omega who fled to Sanctuary. He's in custody now."

The information penetrates the fog of my heat. "The rabbit?"

"A warning. He blamed you for harboring runaways. For teaching their children." His voice hardens. "He won't touch you. I swear it."

The fierce protection in his tone sends another rush of warmth through me—different from the heat, deeper somehow.

"Thank you," I whisper.

Our eyes lock across the classroom. The air between us pulses with unspoken words, with want barely contained. With recognition.

"Jenny," he says, my name almost a prayer on his lips. "I would never—I need you to know I would never—"

"I know." And I do. Despite our differences, despite everything, I trust this truth: Finn Donovan would cut off his own arm before hurting me.

Minutes stretch like hours as we wait, locked in this exquisite torture. Me, burning from the inside out. Him, rigid with restraint, watching over me like a sentinel.

When Olivia's quick knock finally comes, Finn's relief is palpable. He cracks the door, exchanging brief words with her before stepping aside to let her in. The fresh air from the hallway momentarily dilutes the thick cloud of pheromones.

"I've got her," Olivia says softly to Finn. "You should go."

He hesitates, eyes finding mine one last time. Something passes between us—an unspoken promise, a recognition of what almost happened. What still might.

Then he's gone, the door clicking shut behind him.

Olivia helps me to my feet, her omega scent soothing compared to the overwhelming pull of Finn's alpha presence. As she guides me toward her car, I glance back at the school building.

Through the window of my classroom, I catch a glimpse of him—still there, watching, making sure I get away safely. Standing guard like the wolf he is, protecting what he can't yet claim.

What's his. What's always been his, whether I've been ready to admit it or not.

# 7

Twelve hours into my heat, and I'm losing my mind. Olivia got me home safely, set up cooling packs, left suppressants by my bedside, and stationed another omega—Sarah from the bakery—outside my door for safety. The suppressants have taken the edge off, but they can't touch the core of this fire. My whole body pulses with each heartbeat, sheets soaked with sweat and slick. I've weathered heats before—always alone, always in control—but never like this. Never with the image of amber eyes burning behind my eyelids. Never with one name repeating like a prayer in my mind: Finn. Finn. Finn.

I press a cold washcloth to my forehead, trying to think through the fog of pheromones and need. The digital clock on my nightstand reads 2:17 AM. Outside, rain patters against my window, the soft rhythm both soothing and maddening against my hypersensitive skin.

This isn't working. The suppressants, the cooling packs, the breathing exercises—none of it touches this bone-deep ache. My body knows what it wants. Who it wants. The mate bond, half-formed but undeniable, pulls at something deep inside me. I've been fighting it for weeks, denying what was happening between us. Telling myself it was just biology, just chemistry, just convenient proximity to a compatible alpha.

But in this raw, stripped-down state, I can't maintain the lie. This isn't just any heat, and Finn isn't just any alpha. What's happening between us is rare, precious, and terrifying.

I've built my life around independence. Came to Sanctuary to teach, yes, but also to escape the suffocating expectations of traditional pack dynamics. To be valued for my mind, my work, my heart—not just my omega status. I've avoided serious relationships precisely because I feared this—being reduced to biology, to instinct over choice.

But what if it could be both? What if choosing to follow this pull isn't surrendering my autonomy, but exercising it in its purest form?

I reach for my phone, fingers trembling so badly I can barely navigate to his number. I hesitate, thumb hovering over his name. Am I really doing this? Am I ready for what it means?

A fresh wave of heat crashes through me, drawing a whimper from my throat. Beyond the physical need, something deeper aches—a soul-level loneliness that I've carried for so long I'd stopped noticing its weight until now, when the possibility of its absence looms so close.

I make the call before I can talk myself out of it.

He answers on the first ring, voice rough with concern. "Jenny? Are you okay?"

"No." My voice sounds foreign to my own ears—raw, desperate. "I need you. Please."

A sharp intake of breath. "The suppressants—"

"Aren't enough." I close my eyes, forcing myself to say what I need to say. "I want you, Finn. Only you."

Silence stretches between us, taut with possibility.

"Jenny," he says finally, my name a rough caress. "I need you to be sure. This isn't—I can't—"

"I'm choosing this," I tell him, the words steadying me. "I'm choosing you."

Another pause, briefer this time. "Twenty minutes."

The call ends. I let the phone fall to the tangled sheets, my heart thundering against my ribs. Twenty minutes to prepare—as if anything could prepare me for what's coming. I force myself out of bed on wobbly legs, stumbling to the bathroom. The face that greets me in the mirror is flushed, eyes dilated, hair a wild tangle around my shoulders. I look feral, desperate.

I look like an omega in heat. But beneath the physical signs, I still see myself—Jenny Wilson, kindergarten teacher, stubborn defender of the vulnerable. The woman who stood toe-to-toe with the most intimidating deputy in Sanctuary and refused to back down.

That woman is still here, still making choices. Still in control, even as she chooses to let go.

I manage a quick shower, the cool water offering momentary relief against my burning skin. Clean sheets feel like a lost cause, but I change into a simple cotton nightdress—more dignified than the sweat-soaked tank top and underwear I've been writhing in.

Sarah knocks softly, concern in her voice. "Jenny? Someone's here for you. A deputy. Should I..."

"Let him in," I call back, my voice steadier than I expected. "It's okay. I asked him to come."

I hear murmured voices, then footsteps approaching my bedroom. A soft knock, though the door stands ajar.

Finn fills the doorway, his broad shoulders seeming to block out the rest of the world. He's still in uniform, as if he came straight from patrol. His scent hits me like a physical blow—cedar and smoke and alpha need, making my knees buckle. I sink to the edge of the bed, unable to stand under the weight of his presence.

"Jenny." Just my name, but the way he says it—reverent, hungry, careful—contains universes.

He steps into the room but maintains his distance, still fighting his instincts even now. Rain patters against the windows, the only sound beyond our rapid breathing.

"You should know," he says, voice strained, "if we do this... for me, it won't be casual. I can't—"

"I know." I meet his eyes directly, letting him see the clarity behind the heat-haze. "I've felt it too. The bond."

Something shifts in his expression—hope breaking through the restraint. "You have?"

"Yes." I stand on shaking legs, taking a step toward him. "I've been fighting it. I was afraid it would... diminish me somehow. That I'd lose myself in you."

He doesn't move, letting me come to him. "And now?"

"Now I'm choosing it." Another step closer. "I'm choosing you, Finn Donovan. Not because my heat demands it. Not because fate decided it. Because I want you. All of you. The growly deputy. The protective alpha. The man who stood guard at my classroom door and didn't take a single step toward me when every instinct told you to."

His control visibly fractures with each word, with each step I take toward him. When I'm close enough to feel the heat radiating from his body, I stop.

"I'm choosing this," I whisper one last time.

Something breaks in him—the final thread of restraint snapping. He reaches for me with a groan that sounds torn from his very core, hands gentle despite the desperate hunger in his eyes. When his fingers finally touch my skin, it's like a circuit completing. Electricity races through me, igniting every nerve ending.

"Finn," I breathe against his mouth, and then we're kissing—deep, desperate, devastating. His hands cradle my face like I'm something precious even as his body presses mine toward the bed with unmistakable intent. I pull at his uniform shirt, desperate to feel his skin against mine.

"Slow," he murmurs against my throat, even as his hands slide beneath my nightdress. "Let me take care of you."

He keeps his promise—treats me as something breakable and infinitely precious, not a conquest to be claimed. Even as the air between us turns wild with want, every touch is a question, every caress a careful answer. He holds my face between trembling hands, eyes searching mine for the smallest shadow of doubt, as if my need might flicker and die if he presses too hard. But I burn for him, for this, and I bury my fingers in his hair to anchor him to me, drawing him down with a gasp that is both permission and plea.

The first brush of his mouth is impossibly gentle, a worship rather than a devouring. His lips trace the line of my jaw, the hollow behind my ear, learning me as if I am a puzzle he's waited his whole life to solve. His hands map the terrain of my body with reverence, avoiding the places that ache until my skin prickles with anticipation, until the absence of his touch there is its own exquisite torment. I didn't know it could feel like this—like surrender and sovereignty at once, as if I am both swept away by the current and steering the river.

We move together, clothed at first in the barriers of our separate lives—his uniform shirt, my thin nightdress—but as the heat overtakes us, those layers fall away in slow, uncertain increments. He unbuttons his shirt so slowly I want to scream, his hands shaking as if he's terrified the spell will break. I reach for the buttons myself, impatient, but he gently folds my hands back to my sides, eyes meeting mine with a command I want to obey more than I want to breathe.

"Let me," he says, and the words are everything I need.

He kneels on the floor beside the bed to slip the dress over my head, mouth following the path of bare skin as it's revealed. His hands come to rest on my thighs, patient and steady, even as the muscles in his forearms cord with the effort of restraint. I can feel his need, sharp and relentless, but he will not take even a single inch more than I offer. The discipline is a kind of agony, but it's also a gift—a reminder that this is my choosing, always.

When he finally kisses me again, it's different—darker, hungrier, edged with something close to desperation. I taste the storm of his want, the way he's holding it back for my sake, and the power of it makes me lightheaded. I want to give in, give up, let him drown us both. But I also want to savor this moment, to remember every second of how it feels to be seen and wanted and respected all at once.

He slides his hands up my sides, thumbs brushing the undersides of my breasts, and I arch into his touch, shameless in my need.

"Please," I whisper, and the word shatters whatever was left of his composure.

His mouth finds mine, hungry and soft, and the next thing I know we're tangled together on the bed, limbs and need and heat blurring the rest of the world away. Rain drums harder on the windows, as if the night itself is bearing witness.

He parts my knees with a gentle nudge, settling between them with a reverence that undoes me. Even now, as the mate bond throbs between us—no longer a whisper but a roar—he checks in, pausing, searching my face. "Jenny, are you—"

"I need you," I say, and it's the purest truth I have ever spoken.

He groans, low and broken, and finally, finally, he's inside me. The sensation is overwhelming—stretch and slide and the heady rush of belonging. We move together, finding a rhythm that feels ancient and inevitable, as if our bodies remember each other from some other life. His scent saturates the room, familiar and wild, and I breathe it in like oxygen, like absolution.

With every thrust, the bond tightens between us, thickening into something tangible. His hand comes up to cradle my cheek, thumb brushing away the tears I didn't know I'd shed. I don't feel weak or small—I feel stripped bare, all defenses gone, and it's the most terrifyingly beautiful thing I've ever known. My body sings with it, nerves sparking, every sensation so heightened I'm not sure where I end and he begins.

He buries his face in my neck, breath hot against my skin. I feel the edge of his teeth, the scrape of canine against the place where a mating mark would go, but he stops himself with a shudder, even now giving me space to choose the moment. The effort costs him—I can feel it in the way his arms tremble, the way his hips stutter against mine. It should scare me, this power I have over him, but instead it makes me love him in a way I never thought possible.

We're both trembling by the time we come apart, undone and remade by the force of it. For a moment there is nothing but the sound of our breathing and the rain, the rest of the world falling away. He doesn't move to leave or roll away—he holds me so close I can feel his heartbeat echoing mine.

When release finally comes, it's not just physical but spiritual—a shattering and remaking. I cry out his name like a benediction, and he buries his face against my neck, teeth grazing my mating gland but not breaking the skin. Even now, at the height of our joining, he gives me choice.

Afterward, we lie tangled together, my head on his chest, his heartbeat strong and steady beneath my ear. His fingers trace patterns on my bare shoulder, gentle and possessive at once. My heat has quieted to a gentle simmer, satisfied in a way suppressants never managed.

"I've been running from this," he admits into the darkness, voice low and intimate. "From you. From what I felt happening between us."

I tilt my face up to see him. "Why?"

His arms tighten around me. "Because I've seen what happens when alphas claim mates out of instinct rather than choice. My father—" He stops, jaw tightening. "I couldn't bear to trap you that way. To take your freedom."

I press my palm against his cheek, feeling the day's stubble rough against my skin. "You haven't taken anything I haven't freely given."

His eyes—amber and gold in the dim light—search mine for truth. Whatever he sees there makes something in him relax, the last of his defenses falling away.

"I've never felt anything like this," he confesses. "Like I found something I didn't even know was missing."

I settle back against his chest, listening to the steady rhythm of his heart. For the first time since my heat began—perhaps for the first time in years—I feel completely at peace. Complete.

I haven't lost myself in choosing him. I've found parts of myself I didn't know were waiting to be discovered.

"Sleep," he murmurs, pressing a kiss to my forehead. "I'll be here when you wake up."

As I drift toward sleep in his arms, I know with bone-deep certainty that this—us—was always meant to be. Not because fate dictated it, but because we chose it. Each other. This bond. This life we're about to build together.

**8**

—·—

Three days after my heat breaks, I return to school with our bond humming beneath my skin like a live wire. Everything feels different—colors sharper, sounds clearer, my body more present in the world. Finn's scent clings to me despite a thorough shower, marking me as claimed.

As his.

The thought sends a shiver of something between pride and defiance down my spine. I've chosen this bond, but I'm still me—still Jenny Wilson, kindergarten teacher, still determined to make my own way. Now I just happen to have an overprotective alpha deputy sleeping in my bed.

The morning passes in a blur of finger paintings and phonics lessons. My students seem oblivious to the change in me, though Olivia gives me a knowing smile when we pass in the hallway. News travels fast in Sanctuary. By now, everyone must know that Deputy Hard-Ass and the stubborn kindergarten teacher have formed a mate bond.

Just before lunch, my classroom phone rings—Olivia's extension.

"Jenny," she says without preamble, her voice tight with controlled tension. "Code yellow. Now."

My heart stutters. Code yellow—possible threat, precautionary lockdown. I hang up without replying and turn to my class with a deliberately calm smile.

"Boys and girls, we're going to play the quiet game now," I announce, using the code phrase we've practiced. "Everyone please line up quickly at the cubbies."

Twenty-six pairs of eyes look up at me. They don't know what's happening, but they sense my tension. Little Tommy's lower lip trembles as he slides from his chair. I give him a reassuring wink, keeping my movements smooth and unhurried as I guide them to our designated shelter spot—the reading nook in the far corner, away from windows and doors.

"Miss Jenny?" Lily tugs at my cardigan as we hunker down. "Is it the bad man again?"

News travels among children too, it seems. I smooth her hair back from her forehead. "Don't worry, sweetie. The sheriff and Deputy Donovan are keeping us safe."

As if summoned by his name, my phone vibrates with a text from Finn.

> Stay inside. Clarke released on bail.
> Spotted near school grounds.

My blood runs cold. Clarke—the alpha who left the mutilated rabbit. Released. Here.

Through the classroom window, I catch movement in the parking lot—Finn's squad car screeching to a halt, followed by Sheriff Rawlins' truck. They exit their vehicles with the coordinated precision of predators, weapons drawn but held low.

I should pull the blinds, focus only on keeping my students calm. Instead, I find myself riveted to the window, watching as Finn moves with lethal grace across the asphalt. His face is a mask of cold determination, nothing like the man who held me so tenderly three nights ago. This is Deputy Donovan, protector of Sanctuary.

"Everyone pick a book to read quietly," I instruct the children, my eyes still fixed on the scene unfolding outside. "I'll be right back."

I cross to the door, making sure it's locked, then return to the window. More vehicles have arrived—town council members, other deputies, even Mr. Peterson from the hardware store with what looks suspiciously like a hunting rifle. The community is rallying, forming a protective circle around the school.

A figure emerges from the tree line—tall, rangy, with the aggressive stance of a dominant alpha.

Clarke. Even from this distance, his body language broadcasts fury and entitlement. Finn and Sheriff Rawlins approach him, positioning themselves directly between the intruder and the school building.

I can't hear what's being said, but I see Clarke gesturing wildly, jabbing a finger toward the school. Toward my classroom specifically. My skin crawls with the knowledge that I'm his target—not for myself, but for what I represent. Sanctuary's protection of fugitive omegas. The education of children who've escaped controlling packs.

A primal instinct urges me to go out there, to stand with them, to defend what's mine. The mate bond thrums with alarm, sensing Finn's proximity to danger. My fingers twitch with the need to act rather than observe.

But behind me sit twenty-six children who need me here, calm and present. I breathe through the urge to run outside, forcing myself to trust Finn, to trust Sanctuary.

The confrontation escalates. Clarke lunges forward suddenly, something glinting in his hand. Before I can even process the danger, Finn moves—faster than should be possible, a blur of controlled violence. Clarke hits the ground hard, Finn's knee in his back, cuffs snapping around his wrists. The entire takedown lasts maybe three seconds.

I exhale a breath I didn't realize I was holding.

Sheriff Rawlins collects whatever weapon Clarke was holding, securing it before helping Finn haul the man to his feet. The gathered townspeople close ranks around them, escorting Clarke to a waiting patrol car. Not just law enforcement, but ordinary citizens—the baker, the librarian, the retired schoolteacher who walks her dog past my cottage every morning. Sanctuary, living up to its name.

Only after Clarke is secured in the vehicle does Finn look up toward my window. Even at this distance, I feel the intensity of his gaze like a physical touch. The bond between us pulses with relief, with reassurance, with something deeper I'm not quite ready to name.

I raise my hand in a small wave. He nods once, a gesture loaded with meaning. One that says, "I've got you. You're safe. We're safe."

"Miss Jenny?" Tommy's small voice pulls me back to the classroom. "Is the bad man gone now?"

I turn from the window, kneeling to meet his worried eyes. "Yes, sweetie. The bad man is gone. Deputy Donovan and Sheriff Rawlins took him away."

"Deputy Donovan is your special friend now, right?" Zack pipes up from the reading circle. "My mom says he looks at you like my dad looks at her."

Heat rises to my cheeks.

"Deputy Donovan helps keep all of us safe," I reply, diplomatically sidestepping the question. "Now, who wants to read 'Where the Wild Things Are'?"

Twenty minutes later, the all-clear sounds. I lead my class to the cafeteria for a delayed lunch, keeping a watchful eye for any lingering signs of distress. They bounce back quickly, the resilience of children never ceasing to amaze me.

I'm helping Lily open her juice box when a ripple of awareness passes through the lunchroom. Children's heads turn toward the entrance, conversations quieting. I don't need to look to know who's arrived—the bond tells me, humming with proximity, with connection.

Finn stands in the doorway, uniform still immaculate despite the earlier confrontation. His eyes scan the room, landing on me with laser focus. He crosses to our table, nodding politely to the other teachers who watch with poorly concealed interest.

"Miss Wilson," he says formally, though his eyes say something else entirely. "Everything secure here?"

"All good, Deputy." I match his professional tone while my pulse races traitorously. "The children are fine."

He crouches down to our table level, addressing my students directly. "You all did a great job staying safe today."

They stare at him with wide, admiring eyes. Tommy, bolder than the rest, asks, "Did you catch the bad guy?"

A ghost of a smile touches Finn's lips. "We did. He won't be bothering your school again."

"Because you're the strongest," Lily declares with absolute certainty.

Finn's eyes flick to mine, something soft and almost vulnerable passing through them.

"Because Sanctuary protects its own," he corrects gently.

When he rises, his hand brushes mine briefly—a touch that might appear accidental to observers but sends electricity racing up my arm.

"I'll be outside until dismissal," he says, low enough that only I can hear. "Just to be sure."

I nod, throat suddenly tight with emotion. "Thank you."

As he walks away, I feel the weight of what's happened settling around me. Not just the threat and its resolution, but the way the town came together. The way Finn stood between danger and what he considers his to protect. The way I instinctively included myself in that circle of protection—not as someone to be sheltered, but as part of the sheltering force itself.

This town, this pack, these people—they're mine now in a way they weren't before. And I am theirs.

Not because a mate bond dictates it, but because I've chosen to stand with them. To belong.

After school, I find Finn leaning against his cruiser in the parking lot, waiting as the last parents collect their children. When the lot finally empties, I approach him, suddenly shy despite everything we've shared.

"You okay?" he asks, eyes scanning me for any sign of distress.

"I'm fine." I step closer, into his space. "You were incredible today."

He shrugs, uncomfortable with the praise. "Just doing my job."

"No," I contradict softly. "It was more than that. You protected everyone. The whole town came together."

His expression softens as he reaches out to tuck a strand of hair behind my ear. "That's Sanctuary. We take care of our own."

"Take me home?" I ask, reaching for his hand.

His fingers intertwine with mine, the touch grounding and electric at once.

"Always," he says, and in that single word, I hear the promise that extends far beyond this moment, this day, this crisis now passed.

Sanctuary stands united once more. And I stand with it, claimed and claiming in equal measure.

**9**

Something shifts between us the morning after Clarke's arrest. I wake to find Finn already dressed, standing at my bedroom window with his back to me, shoulders rigid with some tension I can't name. When I reach for him across our newly formed bond, I hit a wall—not severed, but deliberately muted.

"Everything okay?" I ask, sitting up, sheets pooling around my waist. He turns, offers a smile that doesn't reach his eyes, and says he's late for work. The kiss he presses to my forehead feels like goodbye.

I tell myself I'm imagining things. We're new to this—to being bonded, to sharing space and scent and lives. Of course there will be adjustments, moments of uncertainty.

But the distance grows over the next few days, spreading like frost across glass. Finn works late, avoids eye contact, responds to questions with clipped answers. He still comes to my bed at night, still holds me as I fall asleep, but there's a hesitancy to his touch that wasn't there before. The bond between us feels stretched thin, a rubber band pulled to its limit.

By the fifth day, I can't ignore it anymore. I wake to find his side of the bed empty again, a hastily scrawled note on the pillow: *Early shift. Don't wait up.*

I sit in my kitchen, staring at the coffee he made before he left—the only evidence he was here at all. The mug warms my palms as I try to understand what's happening. The mate bond thrums between us, undeniable but increasingly one-sided. I can feel him pulling away, retreating behind walls I didn't know existed.

Did I misread everything? Was the intensity between us just the heat, just biology and pheromones driving us together? I thought we'd moved past that, chosen each other deliberately.

No. I refuse to believe that. What we shared—what we're still sharing, despite his withdrawal—is real. And I'm done giving him space to work through whatever crisis he's having on his own.

I dump the coffee down the drain, suddenly furious. I didn't fight my way to independence, build a life on my own terms, just to let some alpha shut down on me without explanation. We're either partners in this bond or we're nothing.

I dress in record time, choosing a sundress in a shade of blue Finn once said brought out my eyes. Not that I'm trying to influence him, of course. Just reminding him what he's pulling away from.

The sheriff's station sits at the center of town, a sturdy brick building with an American flag flapping lazily in the morning breeze. I stride through the front doors, ignoring the curious glances from the dispatcher. Without asking permission, I walk straight back to the bullpen where I know I'll find him.

Finn sits at his desk, head bent over paperwork, looking exhausted. He hasn't been sleeping well either, then. Good. At least I'm not suffering alone.

He senses me before he sees me—his head jerks up, nostrils flaring as he catches my scent. Several emotions flash across his face in rapid succession: surprise, longing, and then that careful blankness that's been driving me crazy.

"Jenny." He rises from his chair, glancing awkwardly at his colleagues who suddenly seem very interested in their computer screens. "What are you doing here?"

"We need to talk." I keep my voice steady despite the storm brewing inside me.

"I'm working."

"I don't care."

A muscle jumps in his jaw. He gestures toward a small conference room off the main area. "Five minutes."

The room smells of coffee and stale donuts. I cross my arms as he closes the door behind us, boxing us into a space barely big enough for a table and four chairs. The proximity makes his scent overwhelm me—cedar and smoke and the undercurrent of sadness that's been clinging to him lately.

"What's going on with you?" I demand without preamble.

He runs a hand through his hair, a rare gesture of uncertainty. "Nothing's going on. I've been busy with the Clarke case."

"Bullshit." The word snaps between us like a whip. "You've been pulling away since the morning after his arrest. The bond—I can feel you shutting me out."

"I'm not—"

"Don't lie to me, Finn." My voice breaks slightly. "Not after everything. Not after what we shared."

He turns away, bracing his hands on the back of a chair, knuckles white with tension. "It's complicated."

"Then uncomplicate it for me." I step closer, fighting the urge to touch him, to bridge this new chasm between us. "Because from where

I'm standing, it looks like you're having second thoughts. About us. About me."

"That's not it." He turns back, and the raw pain in his eyes stops me cold. "It's not about second thoughts. It's about what happens six months from now, a year from now, when you realize this wasn't really your choice."

I blink, confused. "What?"

"Your heat, Jenny. You chose me in the middle of your heat, when biology was screaming at you to find an alpha. Any alpha."

Understanding dawns, followed quickly by indignation. "You think I only wanted you because of my heat? That what we shared wasn't real?"

"I think," he says carefully, "that heat bonds are powerful things. They can make people feel connections that wouldn't exist otherwise."

The hurt cuts deep, but beneath it, I finally see what's happening. He's not rejecting me—he's afraid I'll reject him when the biological imperative fades.

"You idiot," I whisper, taking another step toward him. "My heat didn't create feelings that weren't there. It just lowered my defenses enough to admit what I'd been fighting for weeks."

His gaze is wary, hopeful, terrified. "You can't know that for sure."

"I can." I close the distance between us, standing close enough to feel his warmth but not touching him yet. "Because I've been falling for you since that first day on the playground, when you showed up all alpha authority and tried to intimidate me. I've been fighting it every step of the way because you represented everything I thought I didn't want."

His breath catches. "And what was that?"

"An alpha who thought he knew best. Who led with dominance instead of understanding. Who made me feel things I wasn't ready to feel." I reach up, finally allowing myself to touch his face, feeling the stubble rough against my palm. "But that wasn't really you at all, was it?"

He leans into my touch, eyes closing briefly. "I never meant to make you feel diminished."

"You didn't. You challenged me. Frustrated me. Made me question myself sometimes. But you never once made me feel less." My thumb traces his cheekbone. "My heat didn't create this bond, Finn. It just revealed what was already there."

The wall he's built between us in the bond begins to crumble. I feel him reaching back, tentative at first, then with growing certainty.

"I'm terrified," he admits, voice low and rough. "Not of the bond. Of how much you matter. Of how much I could hurt you. Of failing you."

My heart breaks and mends all at once. This strong, stubborn man who faces down threats without flinching is undone by the fear of causing me pain.

"Then stop running." I take his hand, placing it over my heart so he can feel its steady beat. "We both deserve this, Finn. We both deserve to be chosen, to be wanted. Not by fate or biology or circumstance, but by each other."

He pulls me to him then, his arms wrapping around me with desperate need. I breathe him in, feeling the bond between us bloom wide open again—no barriers, no walls, just the pure connection of alpha and omega who have chosen each other against all odds.

"I'm sorry," he murmurs against my hair. "I thought I was protecting you."

"I don't need protection from this." I tilt my face up to his. "From anything else, maybe. But not from us."

When he kisses me, it feels like coming home after a long absence. The mate bond sings between us, stronger for having been tested. Behind him, through the glass window of the conference room, I catch sight of Sheriff Rawlins rolling his eyes with fond exasperation before tactfully herding curious deputies away from their vantage point.

"Everyone's watching," I whisper against Finn's mouth.

"Let them." His smile—the first real one in days—transforms his face. "Let the whole damn town see that I'm yours and you're mine."

"By choice," I remind him.

"By choice," he agrees, and kisses me again.

# 10

— • —

"I don't need an escort to my classroom, Finn," I say the next morning, watching him pull on his uniform shirt. After yesterday's confrontation and reconciliation at the sheriff's office, he came home with me, and we spent the evening rebuilding bridges, relearning each other's bodies, reinforcing the bond that had strained but never broken. Now, as sunlight streams through my bedroom window, he's insisting on accompanying me to school. "The threat is gone. Clarke's in custody."

"It's not about Clarke." He fastens his belt, the holster settling against his hip with practiced ease. "It's about doing this properly."

"Doing what properly?"

His eyes meet mine in the mirror as he adjusts his collar. "Presenting ourselves to the community. As bonded mates."

Something warm unfurls in my chest. After his doubts, his fears about trapping me, this public declaration means more than he can know. Still, I can't resist teasing him.

"Deputy Donovan, are you planning to parade me around town like some trophy omega?"

He turns, eyebrow raised. "Would you let me if I tried?"

"Not a chance."

His smile—still rare enough to make my heart skip—transforms his face. "Exactly why I'd never try." He crosses the room, pulling me against him. "I just want to walk into that school with you. Let everyone see that the omega who stood up to me, challenged me, drove me absolutely crazy... chose me."

Put like that, how can I refuse?

The drive to school feels different with him beside me, our scents mingling in the enclosed space of his SUV. The mate bond hums contentedly, like a cat in sunlight. I catch him glancing at me as he drives, something possessive and wondering in his gaze.

"What?" I ask, suddenly self-conscious.

"Nothing." His hand finds mine across the console. "Just still can't believe you're real."

The parking lot is busy when we arrive, parents dropping off children, teachers hurrying to their classrooms. Heads turn as Finn helps me from the vehicle, his hand settling protectively at the small of my back. The gesture should feel presumptuous, alpha-typical. Instead, it grounds me.

Olivia meets us at the entrance, her knowing smile making me blush. "Deputy Donovan. What a surprise to see you escorting our Miss Wilson this morning."

"Sheriff thought it would be good to maintain a presence for a few days," he says, the professional excuse fooling exactly no one. "Just a precaution."

"Of course." Her eyes dance with amusement. "The safety of our staff is paramount."

We make our way down the hallway toward my classroom. Whispers follow in our wake, but they're not unkind. Sanctuary understands mate bonds. Respects them. Celebrates them, even. Especially when they form between people already part of the community.

My classroom door is decorated with spring flowers made from construction paper, each bearing a student's name. Finn pauses to study them.

"You made these with them?"

I nod, surprised by his interest. "Art project last week. They're learning about plant life cycles."

Something softens in his expression. "You're good with them. The kids." He looks almost shy. "I've always thought so, even when we were arguing about discipline approaches."

Before I can respond, the first bell rings. Students will be arriving any minute. I unlock my door, stepping into the familiar space that feels somehow new with Finn beside me. He looks out of place among the tiny desks and colorful posters—too tall, too serious, too unmistakably alpha in a space designed for children.

Yet as my students begin trickling in, something remarkable happens. Instead of shrinking from his presence as they did during our first encounter, they swarm him like a hero returned from battle.

"Deputy Donovan!" Tommy reaches him first, small arms wrapping around Finn's leg without hesitation. "Did you bring your police car?"

"You caught the bad man!" Lily declares, looking up at him with undisguised adoration.

"Do you have your handcuffs?" Zack asks, always focused on the equipment.

I watch, stunned, as Finn crouches down to their level, his expression gentling in a way I've only seen directed at me. Gone is the stern deputy who intimidated them on the playground. In his place is a patient, attentive alpha responding to each question with surprising seriousness.

"Yes, I brought my car. Yes, the bad man is locked up where he can't bother anyone. And no, Zack, I won't let you try on the handcuffs, but you can look at my badge if you want."

The children cluster around him, asking questions, touching his uniform with curious fingers. He answers each one, his patience seemingly infinite. When Lily mentions she wants to be a police officer someday, he tells her she'd make an excellent one. When Tommy confesses he's still scared sometimes, Finn assures him that being brave doesn't mean never feeling fear.

I busy myself preparing for the day's lessons, stealing glances at the unexpected scene unfolding in my classroom. This is a side of Finn I'm still discovering—the gentleness beneath the gruff exterior, the care he takes with vulnerable things.

The final bell rings, signaling the start of classes. Finn rises from his crouch, ushering the children toward their desks with surprising effectiveness. As they scramble to their seats, Lily approaches him one last time, her shoelace trailing.

Without prompting, he kneels again, his large hands deftly tying the pink sneaker. "There you go. Double knot so it stays."

"Thank you," she says solemnly. Then, with a child's directness: "Miss Jenny smells like you now. Are you gonna be her husband?"

Heat floods my cheeks as Finn glances up at me, a smile playing at the corners of his mouth. "Something like that," he tells her. "If she'll put up with me."

"She will," Lily says with absolute certainty. "She likes you lots. Her heart goes fast when you come in."

I could die of embarrassment on the spot. Finn rises, looking entirely too pleased with himself. "Does it now?"

"Out," I mouth at him, pointing to the door before my entire class can divulge more observations about my physiological responses to his presence.

He chuckles, a sound I'm still getting used to hearing from him. "I'll be back at dismissal," he tells me, loud enough for the children to hear.

"We'll walk you to your car, Deputy!" Tommy volunteers, and several other students nod eagerly.

When Finn leaves, the room feels both emptier and somehow fuller. Twenty-six pairs of eyes turn to me expectantly.

"Miss Jenny," Zack says, voicing what they're all thinking, "Deputy Donovan is your special alpha now, isn't he?"

There's no use denying what they can plainly scent. "Yes," I admit. "He is."

Their collective reaction is immediate and enthusiastic approval, as if I've done something particularly clever. The rest of the morning passes in a blur of math exercises and reading circles, but beneath it all runs a current of something new—a sense of expanded belonging.

At lunch, Olivia slides into the seat across from me in the teachers' lounge. "The entire town is talking about you two. The way he looked at you in the sheriff's office yesterday…" She fans herself dramatically. "Half the omegas in Sanctuary are swooning."

I roll my eyes, but can't suppress my smile. "He's not always easy, you know."

"The best ones never are." She sips her tea. "But he looks at you like you hung the moon, Jenny. And you look at him the same way, even when you're arguing."

I think about the journey that brought us here—from adversaries to reluctant colleagues to something neither of us saw coming. About how the man I once thought embodied everything I opposed has become the one I can't imagine my life without.

"I never expected this," I confess. "To be so thoroughly part of something. Someone."

"That's Sanctuary for you." Olivia's expression turns thoughtful. "It's not just a place. It's a belonging."

When dismissal time comes, Finn is waiting in the parking lot as promised. True to their word, my students flock around him, forming an impromptu escort as I lock up my classroom. Parents watch with knowing smiles, the town's blessing evident in their nods of approval.

I catch a glimpse of us reflected in the school's glass doors—the deputy and the teacher, surrounded by children, looking for all the world like something that was always meant to be. His life and mine, woven together by choice and fate in equal measure.

The thought should terrify me—the former loner who guarded her independence so fiercely. Instead, it feels like the most natural thing in the world.

**11**

—  ·  —

The honeymoon period of our bond lasts exactly two weeks before the doubts creep in like shadows at dusk. Not about Finn—never about him. About myself. About what it means to be bonded, to be claimed, to be part of a pair after years of fierce independence.

I catch myself second-guessing small decisions: whether to invite friends over without asking him first, whether to stay late at school preparing for the spring concert, whether the clothes I choose send the wrong message about being a bonded omega. Each time I stop, furious with myself. This isn't me. I've never worried about these things. Yet the thoughts persist, whispering beneath the contentment of our bond.

Finn notices—of course he does. He watches me with careful eyes when he thinks I'm not looking, senses my unease through the bond but doesn't push. Instead, he makes a point of asking my opinion more often, creates space for me without being asked, brings home books he thinks I'd enjoy.

Small gestures that say, "I see you. I value you. I'm not trying to change you."

But the fears linger, old wounds from a culture that too often reduces omegas to their biology. I've seen it happen—strong, independent people slowly reshaped to fit into the narrow box of "someone's omega." Sanctuary is different, I know this. But patterns run deep, and this fear has been with me longer than I care to admit.

Saturday afternoon finds me at the Sanctuary Market, shopping list clutched in one hand, mind elsewhere. I'm debating between pasta shapes—a mundane decision that shouldn't require this much contemplation—when a familiar voice breaks through my reverie.

"The bowties are better for catching sauce." Olivia Rawlins appears beside me, shopping basket over one arm. "Though Sheriff swears by penne."

I smile, dropping the bowtie pasta into my cart. "Voice of experience?"

"Three years of marriage to an alpha who has surprisingly strong opinions about Italian food." Her eyes, warm and knowing, study my face. "You doing okay, Jenny? You seem... preoccupied lately."

Something about her gentle concern breaks through my defenses. "Just adjusting," I say vaguely.

She nods toward the café at the front of the store. "Got time for coffee? I could use a break from errands."

Ten minutes later, we sit at a small corner table, steam rising from our mugs. The market café is quiet this time of day—just a few elderly residents playing chess near the window, a young mother nursing a baby in the corner.

"So," Olivia says, stirring sugar into her coffee. "The bond? Or Finn specifically?"

I look up, startled by her directness. "How did you—"

"I've been where you are." She shrugs. "Not exactly the same situation, but close enough. Strong omega, used to handling things alone, suddenly bonded to an alpha with definite opinions about how the world should work."

"It's not that Finn is controlling," I clarify quickly. "He's been nothing but respectful."

"Of course. If he weren't, half the town would be on his doorstep with torches." She smiles. "But that's not the real fear, is it? It's not what he might do. It's what you might become."

The accuracy of her assessment hits like a physical blow. "I've fought so hard to be seen as more than just an omega," I admit. "To be valued for my mind, my work. I don't want to become 'Finn's mate' instead of Jenny Wilson."

Olivia's expression softens. "Before I met Sheriff Rawlins, I was married to an alpha from a traditional pack up north. The kind who believed omegas should be seen and not heard, preferably while pregnant and barefoot." She traces the rim of her mug. "By the time I escaped to Sanctuary, I'd lost so much of myself I barely recognized the woman in the mirror."

I reach across the table, squeezing her hand. I'd known she came to Sanctuary as a refugee, but not the details.

"When I met James—Sheriff Rawlins—I was terrified of repeating the pattern," she continues. "Here was another alpha in a position of authority. Another potential trap."

"What changed?"

Her smile turns wistful. "Time. Patience. Mostly, watching him. Not just with me, but with everyone. The way he listened to people regardless of designation. The way he never used his strength or position to intimidate." She laughs softly. "The way he looked absolutely panic-stricken the first time I scented his interest in me. Like he was the one who should be afraid."

I think of Finn kneeling to tie Lily's shoelace, of the gentle way he answered Tommy's fears, of how he stood guard outside my classroom during my heat rather than taking what biology urged.

"It took a lot for me to accept courtship," Olivia says. "Do you know what I discovered?"

I shake my head.

"That love—real love—doesn't diminish you. It doesn't require surrender. It's not a subtraction, but a multiplication." She leans forward, eyes intent. "I'm not 'just' the Sheriff's omega. I'm Olivia Rawlins, principal, educator, mate, friend. The bond added to who I am. It didn't replace anything."

Her words settle into me like stones dropping through clear water, creating ripples that spread outward. I think about these past weeks with Finn—how he champions my teaching methods now that he's seen them in action, how he asks about my day with genuine interest, how he seems fascinated rather than threatened by my independence.

"Partnership," I murmur. "Not possession."

"Exactly." She finishes her coffee. "The question isn't whether being bonded will change you. Of course it will, just as it changes him. The question is whether those changes expand who you are or contract it."

We finish our shopping together, conversation turning to school matters and town gossip. But her words stay with me, fermenting like wine in the cellar of my thoughts.

When I arrive home, the house smells of garlic and rosemary. Finn stands at the stove, sleeves rolled up, stirring something that makes my stomach growl appreciatively. He glances up as I set the groceries on the counter, his expression warming.

"Hey," he says simply.

"Hey yourself." I move to his side, peering into the pot. "What are you making?"

"That chicken thing you liked at Marge's. I called and bullied the recipe out of her." He looks slightly embarrassed. "No guarantees it's edible."

The gesture—so thoughtful, so unnecessary—floods me with sudden clarity. This man, this alpha who once represented everything I thought I opposed, has been carefully building bridges to me from the first moment of our bond. Not trying to change me or control me, but simply trying to find his way to me.

I reach for his hand, tugging until he faces me fully. "We need to talk."

Alarm flashes across his features. "What's wrong?"

"Nothing's wrong." I lead him to the living room, sitting on the couch and pulling him down beside me. "But I've been wrestling with something, and I need you to hear me out."

He nods, face serious. "I'm listening."

I take a deep breath. "I've been afraid. Not of you, but of losing myself in this bond. In what it means to be 'an alpha's omega' after fighting so hard to be just Jenny."

Pain flickers in his eyes, but he stays silent, letting me finish.

"I realized today that I've been thinking about this all wrong." I take his hands in mine. "I've been seeing love as a kind of surrender, like I have to give up pieces of myself to make room for you. But that's not what this is."

"What is it, then?" His voice is rough with emotion.

"It's choice. It's partnership." I meet his eyes directly. "I'm not choosing this bond because I need you, Finn. I'm choosing it because I want you. Because loving you doesn't make me smaller—it makes me more fully myself than I've ever been."

The tension drains from his shoulders, relief washing across his features. "Jenny..."

"I'm not done." I squeeze his hands. "I choose you. Not because fate decided it or biology demanded it, but because you see me—really see me—and still want me. Because you don't try to dim my light but help it burn brighter."

He pulls me into his arms then, burying his face in my hair. The bond between us pulses with emotion too complex for words—relief, joy, gratitude, love.

"I was so afraid I was taking something from you," he murmurs against my temple.

"You're not taking." I lean back to see his face. "We're both giving. And receiving. That's what makes it work."

His answering smile—open, unguarded—transforms his face. This is the real Finn, the one beneath the stern deputy exterior. The one only I get to see fully.

"For what it's worth," he says, brushing a strand of hair from my face, "I think you've made me better. Softer in the ways I needed to be. Stronger in others."

"We're better together," I agree. "Not because we're alpha and omega, but because we're Finn and Jenny."

His kiss tastes like certainty, like promise, like coming home. The bond between us hums with contentment, no longer something I fear but something I cherish. Something I choose, with eyes wide open and heart fully engaged.

Not surrender, but growth. Not loss, but expansion. Not fate, but love.

Night falls over Sanctuary, wrapping my little cottage in velvet darkness. Finn moves through my kitchen with newfound familiarity, his uniform replaced by soft jeans and a worn t-shirt that does nothing to diminish the authority in his shoulders. I watch him from the doorway, this alpha who stood against a threat for me, who introduced himself to my students, who walked beside me today with pride rather than possession. The mate bond hums between us, no longer strained but strengthened, tempered like steel through fire.

"You're staring," he says without turning, a smile in his voice.

"Can you blame me?" I step behind him, wrapping my arms around his waist, pressing my cheek between his shoulder blades. "It's not every day I get to watch Deputy Hard-Ass make spaghetti in my kitchen."

He turns in my arms, his hands settling on my hips with gentle possession. "I contain multitudes, Miss Wilson."

"So I'm discovering." I reach up, tracing the line of his jaw with my fingertips. The stubble there rasps against my skin, sending shivers racing down my spine.

His eyes darken as he catches the change in my scent—desire unfurling like smoke between us. But there's no urgency to it, no frantic heat-driven need. Just the slow burn of want between two people who have chosen each other.

"Dinner can wait," he murmurs, bending to press his lips to the curve of my neck.

I tilt my head, giving him better access. "You sure? I wouldn't want to ruin your culinary masterpiece."

His laugh rumbles against my skin. "The sauce will simmer. We've got time."

Time. Such a simple word for what stretches before us now—not just hours or minutes, but days, years, a lifetime bound together. The thought should terrify me, this former loner who built walls like fortresses. Instead, it feels like breathing after holding my breath too long.

He takes my hand, leads me toward the bedroom. There's no rush in his movements, no alpha commanding. Just Finn, looking at me like I'm something precious he can't quite believe is his.

In the soft glow of my bedside lamp, we undress each other with careful hands—a deliberate contrast to the frantic tearing of clothes during my heat. He draws my sweater over my head with reverence, his fingertips skimming the bare skin beneath as if memorizing every inch. I work the buttons of his shirt free, pushing it from his shoulders to reveal the topography of scars and muscle that I'm still learning.

"You're beautiful," I tell him, meaning it in ways that go beyond the physical. Beautiful in his stubbornness, his principles, the fierce protection he offers without diminishing me.

Color rises to his cheeks—my strong, confident alpha, undone by simple praise. I press my palm against his chest, feeling his heartbeat strong and steady beneath warm skin.

"Come here," he says, drawing me down onto the bed beside him.

What follows isn't the desperate coupling of my heat, when biology drove us together with a ferocity that left no time for exploration. That was a wildfire, all-consuming, reducing us to instinct and need, burning through the night and leaving us stunned and shaking in the aftermath. This—tonight—is something else entirely, a slow, deliberate discovery of each other. Finn kisses me like he's learning a new language, every touch a careful syllable, every caress a phrase he intends to memorize. His hands map the territory of my body with the patience of a cartographer, tracing familiar and unfamiliar lines, charting the topographies that make me gasp and shudder and arch into his touch. My own fingers are no less curious, skimming over his skin, cataloguing the scars along his ribs, the tense muscle of his back, the places where he is unexpectedly soft.

He breaks away from my mouth, his breath coming in uneven waves as he looks at me—really looks at me, as if he's trying to fix every detail in his memory, to prove to himself it's real. "Tell me what you want, Jenny," he whispers, and it's not a command, just an offering. A safe place to ask for anything.

I want everything. I want to know him with the same thoroughness, to discover the seams and cracks he hides from the world. I want to taste the salt of his skin and the reverence with which he touches me. I want to feel the weight of him and the way he yields, so subtly, when I urge him down onto the mattress. I want to hear the sounds he makes when I scrape my teeth along the sensitive spot behind his ear, to feel the tremor that goes through him when I press my lips to the hollow of his throat. I want to give, not just receive.

He lets me, and more: he invites it. When I slide down, pressing kisses along his sternum, he props himself on his elbows to watch, his eyes dark and hungry and a little awed. I trace his scars with my tongue, asking silent questions, and he answers them all in the way he shivers or sighs or fists his hands in the sheets. When I reach his belt, he stills my hands, just for a moment, his voice gentle but sure. "Look at me."

I do, and the vulnerability in his expression cracks something open inside me. This is a man who has spent his whole life in control—of himself, of the room, of every situation. But here, with me, he lets himself be unguarded. He lets himself want.

He gathers me back to him, rolling us so I'm beneath him, and takes his time reacquainting himself with every inch of my body. It's not the frantic tearing of clothes and tangled limbs from before. It's unhurried, reverent, a worship that feels like a promise. His hands are everywhere—my waist, my thighs, my face, cradling my jaw as if I'm something precious. When he enters me, it's so slow I almost can't stand it, the anticipation a sweet ache that builds and builds. I'm painfully aware of every inch as he slides deeper, connecting us in a way that's shockingly tender.

"I never thought it could be like this," he confesses against my skin, voice rough with emotion. "Finding you. Finding this."

I understand completely. The bond between us pulses with shared wonder—that after everything, all our clashes and misunderstandings, we ended up here. Together. By choice.

He worships my body with a patience that borders on torment—mouth and hands moving with deliberate slowness, coaxing responses I didn't know I was capable of. I tremble beneath him, coming apart in ways that have nothing to do with omega biology and everything to do with the man himself.

"Finn," I gasp as pleasure builds within me, his name both plea and praise.

"I've got you," he murmurs, his eyes never leaving mine. "Always."

When I come undone, it's not that wild, elemental ripping apart that overtook me in heat. It is something quieter, more seismic—a tectonic shift inside me, as if the earth has re-formed itself around this moment, this man, this bond. A bright shock fractures me into trembling pieces; for the first time, I surrender wholly, no battle or argument or performance. My hands fist in the sheets as I cry out, and Finn catches the sound with his mouth, swallowing the evidence of my need as if it could nourish him. The salt of my tears stains his shoulder where I press my face, and he holds tight through every wave, rocking me fiercely through the aftershocks.

He softens his grip only when I slacken, boneless and dazed, and I feel him brush careful thumbs beneath my eyes, gathering whatever tears he finds there. He doesn't speak at first—only holds me, rubbing soothing circles between my shoulder blades, steadying our breath until the world grows quiet again. The silence is not emptiness, but fullness: the hush of two hearts recalibrating. I am so unmoored by it I can hardly remember the woman I was before. There is no shell, no armor, no clever retort left to hide behind. Only flesh and spirit, exposed and remade.

He moves as if maybe he'll stop there, but I am already restless—to give, to match his reverence with my own, to learn every secret of his body as he has mapped mine. I press him backwards on the mattress, and he lets me, eyes wide with something like reverence. I climb astride him, feeling the lingering heat where he'd joined us, and shudder to realize how perfectly we fit. He is heavy and hot between my thighs, still achingly hard. In this light, stripped of uniform and bravado, Finn looks younger, softer, but no less dangerous. I want to devour him, every inch.

I plant my hands on his chest and explore, slow and methodical. My palms skate over muscle and smattering of pale scars—evidence of old fights, old pain, all laid bare for me to see. I duck my head to taste him, tongue finding the ridge of his collarbone, the salt of his skin, the faintest pulse at the base of his throat. I kiss my way down, lingering at the hollow just above his sternum, where his heartbeat thunders so loud I can almost taste it. His breathing hitches, and I feel victorious.

When I dip lower, tracing the ladder of his ribs, he squirms, trying not to show how sensitive he is. I make a point of cataloging every spot that makes him gasp—a patch near his left nipple, a divot by his hip, the paper-thin skin over his inner elbow. I want to know him as thoroughly as he knows me, to file away these facts for future use. He watches me with a gaze that burns, mouth open, hair mussed, hands knotting in the sheets.

I press kisses to the scars along his side, and when I meet his eyes, I see surprise there: as if all his expectations were for his own strength, not for gentleness. He tries to touch me, but I bat his hands away—my turn now. I grasp his wrist, pinning it above his head, and for a second he goes perfectly still, eyes blazing with shock, then surrender. I can see how badly he wants to let go of control, to trust. The realization breaks me open all over again.

I sink lower, lips and teeth and tongue tracing the muscles of his abdomen, biting just hard enough to make him flinch, then soothing the spot with my mouth. I reach his waistband and tug his jeans down, letting him spring free. The sight of him—thick, flushed, already leaking—is intoxicating. I wrap my hand around the base, marveling at the heft and heat, and stroke slowly, savoring how instantly his self-control cracks.

I don't go down on him—not yet. Instead, I slide up his body and lower myself onto him, guiding him inside with a flex of my hips. The stretch is sublime, and for a second we just hold there, locked together, breathing one another in. I brace my hands on his chest and begin to move, rolling my hips in a rhythm that is unhurried and relentless. He groans, head snapping back, the tendons in his neck standing out in sharp relief.

I keep my eyes on him, drinking in every expression—the disbelief, the hunger, the utter captivation. I want him to remember this, to carry it with him like a secret weapon. He tries to thrust up into me, but I pin his hips with my thighs, keeping control. I love the look of frustration and awe mingled on his face, the way he seems desperate to surrender and desperate to resist all at once.

I lean forward, biting his earlobe, whispering all the things I want to do to him, all the ways I want to make him fall apart. My words make him shudder, his hands flexing uncontrollably against the mattress. I can feel him getting close, the tension winding tighter with every pulse. I slow my pace, teasing him, making him beg with his eyes. His voice is hoarse when he speaks, words nearly lost to the growl in his throat.

"Jenny," he warns as I take him in my hand, his control visibly fraying. "I need—"

"I know what you need." I move up his body, guiding him to where I want him most. "I need it too."

We move together, finding a rhythm that feels both new and familiar, as if our bodies remember each other from lives before this one. His hands frame my face, thumbs brushing away tears I didn't know I'd shed.

"You're crying," he says, concern threading through desire. "Should we stop?"

I shake my head, pressing my lips to his palm. "Happy tears. Don't you dare stop."

His answering smile is everything—tender and fierce and entirely mine.

As our movements quicken, the bond between us pulses brighter, stronger. I feel his pleasure as if it's my own, amplifying mine in an endless loop of sensation. His mouth finds my neck, teeth grazing the spot where a mating mark would go—asking without words.

"Yes," I breathe, tilting my head to give him better access. Not submission, but invitation. "Claim me, Finn. Make us complete."

His eyes meet mine, searching for any doubt, any hesitation. "You're sure? This is forever, Jenny."

"I've never been more sure of anything." I cup his face between my hands. "I choose you. Now and always."

The emotion in his eyes nearly undoes me. He presses his forehead to mine, our breath mingling. "I choose you too. My stubborn, beautiful omega."

When release builds again, sweeping through us both like a gathering storm, Finn's teeth find my throat. The sharp sting of the claiming bite sends a shock of pleasure-pain radiating through my entire body. I cry out, nails digging into his shoulders as the bond between us flares incandescent, no longer stretched between two separate beings but fused into something unbreakable.

For a moment, I swear I can feel his heartbeat as my own, his pleasure indistinguishable from mine. The sensation is overwhelming, tears streaming down my face as wave after wave of completion washes through us both.

When awareness returns, Finn is cradling me against his chest, his fingers gentle in my hair. The bite at my throat pulses warm, already healing with preternatural speed as our bond completes itself. I reach up, touching it with wonder.

"Okay?" he asks, voice rough with emotion.

"More than okay." I smile against his skin, feeling the bond between us—no longer a tentative connection but a living thing, binding us together while somehow making us more ourselves. "I feel... whole. Like something was missing and I didn't even know until now."

His arms tighten around me. "I know exactly what you mean."

We lie tangled together, heartbeats gradually synchronizing. Outside, Sanctuary sleeps, unaware that something miraculous has happened within its boundaries tonight. Not just a claiming—those happen often enough—but a choosing. Two people who fought the pull of fate until they realized it was showing them what they most needed: each other.

"Jenny Wilson," Finn murmurs against my hair, "you've ruined me for anyone else, you know that?"

I laugh softly, pressing my lips to the center of his chest. "Good. Because you're stuck with me now, Deputy Donovan."

"Promise?" His voice holds a vulnerability few would ever hear from him.

I raise my head, meeting his eyes in the soft darkness. "Promise."

The mate bond between us hums with contentment, with certainty. With the knowledge that what we've found isn't the end of our independence, but the beginning of something stronger than either of us could be alone.

**13**

—  ·  —

Morning sunlight spills across the kitchen counter, catching on the rim of Finn's coffee mug and the badge he's set beside it. Steam rises in lazy curls as he flips through my lesson plans, red pen in hand, making occasional notes in the margins. Six weeks into our bonded life, and this has become our routine—coffee shared in the quiet morning hours, his uniform pressed and waiting, my classroom materials spread between us. The domesticity of it should chafe against my independent nature. Instead, it feels like the most natural thing in the world.

"You're teaching them about police officers this week?" He taps the community helpers unit plan I've drafted, eyebrow raised.

"Seemed appropriate." I hide my smile behind my mug. "I happen to know a very good example."

"Hmm." He makes another note, his handwriting neat and precise, so at odds with his gruff exterior. "You should add firefighters. And bring in protective gear for them to try on. Kids remember things better through tactile learning."

This is the part that still surprises me daily—how thoroughly he's taken an interest in my work, my students, my teaching philosophy. The man who once argued that fear was educational now suggests gentler approaches, researches childhood development in his spare time, asks thoughtful questions about my methods.

"Sheriff Rawlins would probably let you borrow a child-sized vest from the community outreach closet," he adds, glancing up. The morning light catches in his eyes, turning them to warm honey.

I lean across the counter to kiss him, just because I can. "Look at you, Mr. Educational Theory."

His hand cups the back of my neck, holding me close for a moment longer than necessary. "I have a vested interest in tiny humans being properly educated now."

The bond between us hums with contentment, with rightness. Six weeks, and I'm still discovering new facets of him—the tenderness beneath the gruff exterior, the quick intelligence, the unexpected streak of nurturing that emerges more with each passing day.

My cottage has transformed gradually with his presence. His uniform shirts hang beside my dresses in the closet. His tactical boots sit next to my flats by the door. The bookshelves now hold his dog-eared crime novels alongside my classics and teaching references. Mabel, initially suspicious of this alpha invader, now sleeps curled on his chest every evening.

It's not just my space anymore. It's ours. Our scents mingle in every room, creating something new and uniquely belonging to us.

"Don't forget the pack meeting tonight," Finn reminds me, gathering his things. Sheriff Rawlins hosts monthly gatherings for Sanctuary's core protection team and their mates—part social event, part strategy session for keeping the town safe.

"I'll bring those brownies Olivia likes." I straighten his collar, a gesture that's become habit. "Try not to terrify any speeders today."

"Can't make promises." He kisses me one more time before heading out, pausing at the door. "I might stop by the school at lunch."

The casual statement warms me more than it should. "The kids would love that."

His smile—still rare enough to feel like a gift—flashes briefly. "Just the kids?"

"Maybe their teacher too," I admit. "A little."

After he leaves, I finish getting ready, the house quieter but still filled with his lingering presence. The drive to school feels different now. Sanctuary itself feels different—smaller, warmer, more intimately mine. Streets I've driven for three years suddenly hold new meaning. That's where we had our first real conversation. That's the diner where he finally admitted he was avoiding me. That's the sheriff's station where I confronted him about pulling away.

This town isn't just where I live and work anymore. It's where I found him. Where I found us.

The school day passes in a blur of activity. We're making paper hats representing different community helpers—firefighter, mail carrier, doctor, police officer. Tommy insists on making his police hat extra large, "like Deputy Donovan's."

"Deputy Donovan doesn't wear a hat," Lily corrects him with the supreme confidence of a five-year-old know-it-all.

"He should," Tommy argues. "For protection."

I hide my smile as I help Zack with his scissors. These children, who once cowered from Finn's alpha presence, now argue about his uniform accessories with proprietary familiarity. They've adopted him as their own personal hero, a status he bears with bemused tolerance.

True to his word, Finn arrives during lunch period, slipping into the cafeteria with a nod to the lunch monitors. The children spot him immediately, a ripple of excitement spreading through their tables. He makes his way to where

I'm helping open milk cartons, his hand brushing mine briefly in greeting.

"Deputy Donovan!" Lily abandons her sandwich to show him her paper police badge. "I made it myself!"

"Very official," he tells her seriously. "Good work, Officer Lily."

He settles at our table, immediately swarmed by kindergarteners showing him art projects, telling him stories, competing for his attention. I watch, heart swelling, as this man who once intimidated them with his mere presence now listens to each child with genuine interest. He helps open stubborn juice boxes, wipes spilled milk with efficient care, answers endless questions about his job with patience I never would have attributed to him two months ago.

"You're good with them," I tell him later, as we walk together toward my classroom.

He shrugs, uncomfortable with praise as always. "They're good kids."

"They adore you."

His ears redden slightly. "They're easily impressed."

"No," I correct gently. "They recognize what I see—that beneath all that alpha intimidation is a man who protects what he loves. Who sees them as worth protecting."

His expression softens as he looks down at me. "Worth protecting," he echoes, and I know he's not just talking about the children anymore.

Evening finds us on my porch swing—our porch swing now—watching the sunset paint the sky in shades of pink and gold. Finn's arm curves around my shoulders, my head resting against his chest. Mabel purrs in my lap, the evening air carries the scent of Mrs. Henderson's roses from next door.

"Did you ever think we'd end up here?" I ask, watching a star appear in the darkening sky. "That first day on the playground, when you came storming in with all your rules and regulations?"

His chest rumbles with quiet laughter. "Not in my wildest dreams. I thought you were the most infuriating omega I'd ever met."

"And now?"

"Still infuriating." He presses a kiss to my temple. "But also the best thing that's ever happened to me."

The bond between us pulses with emotion—strong, steady, certain. Not the desperate, consuming fire of those early days, but something deeper, more enduring. A foundation rather than a flash flood.

We sit in comfortable silence as darkness falls fully, porch lights blinking on up and down the street. Sanctuary settling into its evening routine around us.

"Thank you," I say finally.

"For what?"

"For not letting me push you away. For being patient while I figured out what I really wanted. For seeing me—really seeing me."

His arms tighten around me. "I should be thanking you. For standing up to me. For challenging me. For making me a better man."

I think about the journey that brought us here—from adversaries to reluctant colleagues to unexpected mates. About how the universe sometimes gives you exactly what you need in the package you least expect.

Sanctuary has always been a place where broken people come to heal, where fugitives find refuge, where new beginnings are possible. I came here seeking independence, determined to build a life on my own terms. I never expected that true freedom would come from choosing to share that life with someone else.

For the first time in longer than I can remember, I feel completely, utterly at peace. The bond between us, the life we're building, the community that's embraced us—it's more than I dared hope for.

I am loved. I am chosen. I am free.

And in Finn's arms, in this town that has become truly home, I know that our story is just beginning. Whatever comes next, we'll face it together—the cynical deputy and the sunshine teacher who turned out to be exactly what each other needed.

"I love you," I whisper into the gathering darkness.

His kiss is gentle, reverent, certain. "I love you too. Always will."

The mate bond sings between us, a melody that's uniquely ours—harmony found in the most unexpected of places, with the most unexpected of partners.

My happily ever after. Our happily ever after.

Together.

Find out what happens next in Sanctuary with Nate and Lila's story in The Alpha Mayor! (Continue to the next page for a Bonus Epilogue.)

Want more of Ethan and Avery? Sign up for the Ash Jade newsletter and download a free bonus scene today! Click here: The Alpha Mayor Bonus Scene

—·—

# BONUS EPILOGUE

## NATE

The clock on the wall ticks past midnight, each sound scraping against my nerves like claws on stone. I twist Lila Morgan's application between my fingers, the paper soft from handling, her name circled in my neat handwriting. Three times I've read this thing tonight. Three times I've traced that ridiculous cursive L with my eyes. My wolf stirs beneath my skin, restless and wanting. Something I refuse to name.

Everyone else cleared out an hour ago. The building's empty except for me and the hollow echo of my own breathing. The fluorescent lights hum overhead, bathing my cluttered desk in harsh white that makes my eyes ache.

Two hours of budget squabbles and zoning permits. Another hour of Sheriff Hawkins dropping not-so-subtle hints about needing more deputies—like I don't know we're understaffed. Like I haven't been the one fighting the county for more funding.

I roll my shoulders, bones cracking in the silence. At thirty-eight, I shouldn't feel this worn down. Mayor of Sanctuary for seven years now, and some days it feels like I've aged twenty.

The application taunts me from my desk, innocent white paper with that faint trace of something that keeps drawing me back. I grab my pen, tap it against the edge of my desk. Tap. Tap. Tap.

Lila Morgan. Twenty-two. Political science major with a minor in environmental studies. Wants to intern for the summer "to gain practical experience in municipal governance while contributing to Sanctuary's unique community model."

Pretty words. Safe words.

Words that say absolutely nothing about why a young omega would choose this backwoods town for an internship when she could be in Denver or Seattle. Sanctuary doesn't advertise what we really are. Not officially. But omegas know. The whisper network makes sure of that.

I lift the paper to my nose, inhaling deeply. There it is again—that scent. Sweet, but not cloying. Like wild blackberries warmed by the sun. My pupils dilate, and I catch myself growling low in my throat.

"Fuck." I drop the paper like it's burning my fingertips.

This is exactly why I've been putting off making a decision. I've been telling myself it's about security protocols, background checks, the usual bureaucratic bullshit. But it's this—this primal, unwanted reaction to a scent on paper.

My wife's been gone three years. I haven't reacted to an omega's scent since Sarah. Haven't wanted to.

"It's just biology," I mutter to the empty office. "Just pheromones."

I stand abruptly, pacing the worn carpet between my desk and the window. Outside, Sanctuary sleeps under a blanket of stars. Main Street empty except for the occasional flicker of the neon sign above Marge's Diner. The mountains rise black against the night sky, protective giants guarding our borders.

I built this place—not the town itself, but what it represents. A haven for omegas running from abusive packs, from forced bonds, from alphas who think designation equals ownership. We don't advertise it. We don't talk about it. But every deputy, every council member, every business owner in town knows: Sanctuary protects its own.

My personal feelings don't matter here. They can't matter.

The application stares up at me from my desk. I run my fingers through my hair, tugging at the strands until my scalp stings.

An intern. Just an intern. A college student who'll file papers, take notes at meetings, maybe help with the Founder's Day Festival planning. She'll be gone by August, back to whatever university she came from.

So why does my wolf pace anxious circles in my chest?

I check the address on her application again. Boulder. Not surprising. Universities are safer for omegas than most places, but still. Boulder's less than three hours away. Close enough to have heard about Sanctuary, far enough that she's not local.

No pack affiliation listed. Another red flag—omegas without pack protection are vulnerable. Unless she's running from her pack. Wouldn't be the first to show up here with a story about needing work experience when what she really needs is a place no alpha can follow.

I should call Jake. The sheriff's department runs background checks on every new resident, especially omegas who might bring trouble to our door. But it's after midnight, and this isn't an emergency. It can wait until morning.

With a growl of frustration, I slide the application into my "approved" folder. The council will rubber-stamp it—they trust my judgment on these things. And if Lila Morgan is running from something, better she's here where we can protect her than out there alone.

I shut down my computer, straighten my desk, tuck the folder into my briefcase. The routine motions ground me, pull me back from the edge of whatever precipice I was teetering on. Mayor Carrington, responsible alpha, father, widower. The man Sanctuary relies on. Not some feral beast chasing phantom scents.

The hallway lights flicker as I lock my office door. The old building settles around me, creaking like an arthritic joint. Budget meeting next week needs to address the electrical issues. Again. I make a mental note, adding it to the endless list of tasks that define my days.

Outside, the night air hits me like a cold shower. Pine and loam and mountain snow, even in late spring. I fill my lungs, letting the familiar scents of home clear my head. The parking lot is empty except for my truck, black and solid in the moonlight.

The drive home follows roads I could navigate blindfolded. Past the sheriff's department, lights still on because Jake never sleeps. Past Marge's Diner where the overnight cook is probably making pancakes for the truckers passing through. Past the motel where newcomers land before we find them something more permanent.

My headlights catch movement ahead—a car coming from the opposite direction. Not unusual, even at this hour, but something about it makes my hands tighten on the steering wheel. It's not a local vehicle—I know every car in Sanctuary by sight, by sound, by scent.

This one's different. Small. Dark. Moving too fast for these winding roads.

As it passes, something electric shoots through me. A jolt like touching a live wire. My wolf surges forward, clawing at my control, demanding I turn around and follow. I slam on the brakes, the truck skidding slightly on the gravel shoulder.

"What the fuck?" I whisper, heart hammering against my ribs.

I twist in my seat, watching red taillights disappear around the bend. The urge to chase is overwhelming, primitive. I haven't felt anything like this since—

"You're tired," I tell myself. "Working too many hours. Brain playing tricks."

I glance in the rearview mirror one last time, seeing nothing but empty road behind me. Whoever was in that car is heading into town. Probably just passing through. Probably nothing to do with me or Sanctuary or the stack of paperwork waiting for my signature tomorrow.

The moonlight streams through the pines as I pull into my driveway. The house is dark except for the porch light I always leave burning.

Home. Safe. Normal.

But as I climb the porch steps, keys jingling in my hand, I can't shake the feeling that the carefully ordered world I've built is about to shatter. That somewhere between dusk and dawn, fate slipped into Sanctuary like a thief.

And I've left all my doors unlocked.

Ready to find out more? Read Nate and Lila's story in The Alpha Mayor!

## ALSO BY ASH JADE

### Read more from Ash Jade

Short, binge-worthy omegaverse romances where instinct burns hot and love always wins.

### Lost Ridge Riders Universe

**Welcome to Lost Ridge.**
*Where the roads are long, the walls are guarded, and no omega is ever owned—only chosen.*

### Salt and Timber Coast Universe

**Welcome to the Salt & Timber Coast.**
*A rain-bound peninsula where protection is steady, bonds are chosen, and love means staying.*

## Blackwater Bears

*A quiet inland pack where bear shifters offer shelter, endurance, and a home that holds.*

## The Starfall Ridge Quick Reads Series

***Welcome to Starfall Ridge.***
*Where the crater sparks scents, fate strikes fast, and no one escapes the pull of a mate.*

## The Yule Curse Series

*Four fated nights. Four cursed alphas. One winter where heat burns brighter than fire.*

## The Touch Her and Die Series

*In a world ruled by dominance, instinct, and the pull of fate, every story begins with danger—and ends with devotion.*

## <u>The Sanctuary Pack Series</u>

***Welcome to Sanctuary.***

*A hidden mountain town where omegas come to heal—and alphas learn what it means to protect.*

# ABOUT ASH JADE

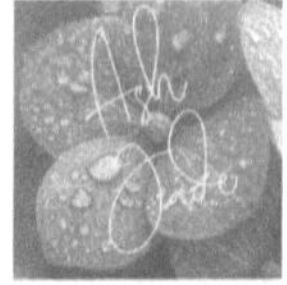

Ash Jade writes trope-packed omegaverse romances full of heat, ruts, and fated mates — but always with heart. Her stories are fast, messy, and addictive, blending primal passion with emotional cores that make the bonds hit even harder. If you love bingeable romances where instinct tangles with feelings (and always ends in happily-ever-after), you've found your pack.

ashjadeauthor.com